REVENGE TACTICS
from the MASTER

GEORGE
HAYDUKE

MW00744737

REVENGE TACTICS from the MASTER

GEORGE HAYDUKE

A Lyle Stuart Book
Published by Carol Publishing Group

Carol Publishing Group Edition - 1994

Copyright © 1993 by George Hayduke
All rights reserved. No part of this book may be reproduced in any form, except by a newspaper or magazine reviewer who wishes to quote brief passages in connection with a review.

Originally published as *More down-and-Dirty Revenge Techniques*

A Lyle Stuart Book
Published by Carol Publishing Group
Lyle Stuart is a registered trademark of Carol Communications, Inc.

Editorial Offices: 600 Madison Avenue, New York, NY 10022
Sales & Distribution Offices: 120 Enterprise Avenue, Secaucus, NJ 07094
In Canada: Canadian Manda Group, P.O. Box 920, Station U, Toronto, Ontario, M8Z 5P9, Canada

Queries regarding rights and permissions should be addressed to:
Carol Publishing Group, 600 Madison Avenue, New York, NY 10022

Manufactured in the United States of America
ISBN 0-8184-0575-9

Carol Publishing Group books are available at special discounts for bulk purchases, sales promotions, fund raising, or educational purposes. Special editions can also be created to specifications. For details contact: Special Sales Department, Carol Publishing Group, 120 Enterprise Ave., Secaucus, NJ 07094

10 9 8 7 6 5 4 3 2 1

Neither the author nor the publisher assumes any responsibility for the use or misuse of information contained in this book.

CONTENTS

¡HASTA LUEGO!

This is a first for me. But, as my friend Bill Grosch is unique and was responsible for many of my honorable values you have read in these pages over the years, I am dedicating this book to him, his family, and to my memories of him.

Bill died in January of 1993, much too soon. On the other hand, perhaps he knew something we don't . . . yet. He always liked to laugh, usually at inappropriate times and subjects, and, perhaps, he is doing so now.

Bill was an artist who believed in art, not manufacture. He was a man of family, of the woods, of the country. He and I plotted sniper attacks and demolition ops against the land rapists who threatened his homestead. It is probably an accident of prudence that they stopped short of his property line, for it was nothing that he and I did actively. Of course not.

A wonderfully sardonic friend, Bill used to tell me how to tend my garden. When I suggested that he tend his own, he'd smile and say, "Oh, that's Phyllis' job." The forever lovely Phyllis, what a grand lady, woman, and friend. She was Bill's perfect counterpoint.

A world-traveled raconteur, Bill packed myriad stories in his experience, all entertaining, all amusing. He would not suffer pompous windbags, though, which always caused me to wonder how he remained a college professor for so many years, that field being infamous for pomposity, windbaggery, and mismanagement.

Bill and I worked at the same institution together briefly, and he is the man who taught me much of my suspicion and mistrust of suitmen. Bill and I also shared that great graduate school of values called the U.S. Army, he during the Korean killing, I a few years later in more tropical lands. But, we had that bond.

We shared another bond a whole lot of years ago. After extended conference with John Barleycorn, Bill and I founded the Oldephart Society of America. The pity is that America failed to recognize our vision. Today, of course, our idea is alive and sort of well at every mall, nursing home, geriatric food booth, and retirement village in the land. Just look around. Bill and I had a pioneering vision of these oldepharts years ago.

We published several newsletters and fought back against our detractors and critics who would have censored our fun and free thought.

John Donne wrote that no man is an island. Yet I loved Bill for the fact that his very persona was a living refutation of John Donne, whose philosophy I have always admired. Bill was an island, and Bill was entirely of himself. And, like me, he refused to be part of the main(stream). I wonder if Bill and John have met yet?

Bill was in Japan a few years ago at the same time Ronald Reagan was on one of his personal greed tours, as opposed to opening for the Rolling Stones. Anyway, one of Bill's old potting compatriots got him a personal audience with the old gentleman. As the two strolled out on the balcony in Tokoyo Square, where the former president was going to address the huddled masses, one of the huddled masses looked up and asked his companion, "Hey, who's that old guy up there with Bill Grosch?"

Not one to let such a magic moment for sensitivity pass, Bill smiled at Reagan and said, "Oh, you'll wonder where the yellow went when we nuke the Orient."

Adios for now, partner. And, as Roy used to sing when we went to those Saturday matinee westerns, "Happy trails to you, until we meet again."

¡Hasta luego, Amigo!

THANK YOU

There are some folks I would like to thank in public for their help, friendship, inspiration, motivation, and/or contributions to my life. This list is in no special order, nor is it inclusive. It's just me saying "thanks."

Ray Heffer, Doug Brunnell, New Age Lady, Ragnar Benson, John Young, Barbara McNeill, E. Park Dietz, Paco Escobar, Don Steffey, John Craig, P.E. Straley, Lee Lapin, Ms. Anonymous, The Brothers McGeary, Karl Bopp, Bigfoot, Marie Leveau, Chris Nemec, Gary Love, Travis Kenneth Bynum I, Dave Hughes, Dick Smegma, Scott French, Hugh Jordan, Lisa Lyon-Lilly, Eugene Mormon, Robert K. Brown, Hugh Troy, John Henry Faulk, Eduardo Zazquez, Paul Markham, Tom Johnson, Ron Anthony, Peder Lund, Jim Kinnon, Alfredo Mussolini, et. al.

OH MY GOD! HE'S BACK

Why am I still here, still writing these books? I tried being an Amway pyramidmeister in the former Soviet Union. I tried to solve world hunger by telling folks to eat their own body wastes—the ultimate recycling, I called it.

I even tried going back to the business world, but I couldn't stand the suits who raced around like they were 20 minutes late for their next shit and a dime short for the pay crapper.

Everywhere in this world I went, I still found really nice people being bullied by very nasty institutions and uncaring other people. Mind over matter, they called it—we don't mind that you don't matter.

I also began to feel the jaws of the New World Order's version of capitalistic democracy clamping steel tight on my poor old ass and figured it was time to follow Mark Twain's advice of "whenever you find that you are on the side of the majority, it's time to reform."

It's just like Franz Kafka's advice that in a fight between you and the world, back the world. So, I figured it was time to blow my cover and come in from the cold world of the grown-ups

World of the grown-ups? Yeah, when you were a kid, they made you color inside the lines. Why? They said you had to follow their rules. Why? Your yesterday's schoolyard bully is today's civic leader or elected thing. And they still push their rules on the rest of us.

There is absolutely no reason for you to have to color inside the lines just because the grown-ups say you had to do so. My old boozin' and war buddy David Hazinski first told me about "the grown-ups" years ago, and he was right. In the same sense, Deli Roo Cahoot told me, "Remember George, only dead fish really swim with the flow."

Grown-ups will tell us that we smell like roses even while we're sitting up to our eyeballs in putrid shit. They'll tell us the streets need to be swept clean, but we can't afford brooms. Fight more wars to get more peace, they'll preach. Keep the motors turning out pollution, but stop using oil. Buy American. Where?

Don't stop asking questions, but do start demanding answers. But do so with a grin. It makes the grown-ups and other bad guys nervous when you grin at them. Just ask my humorous and intelligent editoress, Karen. Coming in a close second in the Cabo World Eructation Finals, Karen gained the Mistress of Vulgarity title, much to the chagrin of the grown-ups. Her associate, the pulchritudinous Tina, poked her metaphorical finger in their eyes by winning the Ms. Temperance title.

Speaking of folks capable of producing a grin for the good and a grimace for the bad, people still ask me if the late Edward Abby was my mentor. While he certainly was my literary genesis, he was not my mentor. That task fell to Ambrose Bierce, who is MIA'd from the Mexican revolution in 1913.

In his last letter home, Mr Bierce wrote "Goodbye If you hear of my being stood up against a Mexican stone wall and shot to rags, please know that it is a pretty good way to depart this life. It beats old age, disease, or falling down the cellar steps. To be a gringo in Mexico, ah, that's euthanasia." Mr. Bierce was 72 when he enjoyed his last round.

How long will my books of terrorizing humor continue? Perhaps someday I will speak to Mr. Bierce about that. Until then, I will keep laughing. And speaking of laughing, it was time for me to do another one of these fun books, and, here we are, together again, naturally.

It's easier to laugh now. In an earlier life, I escaped from a world where recognition was measured in empties, scar tissue, and survival. A lot of my friends were so rough that they wore out their clothes from the inside So, I'd be thrilled if we had a gentle, kind world managed by tree huggers and our police officers could wear shorts and blazers, ride English bicycles, and be happily underutilized. Unhappily, we aren't there and probably never will be as the bullies still vastly outnumber the lotus eaters, even if only in attitude

When I pooped and snooped as one of Uncle's mufti-clad nephews, I worked with two "sergeants" whose names were "Smith," of course. I remember one of them telling me about a couple of the "indigenous personnel" with whom we worked in someone else's country. Here's what he advised: "Never, ever, get on their shit list, George. Those bastards will follow you into hell itself to get their revenge. If you die before they even the score, they'll dig up your body and piss all over it. If it takes till the day after forever, they'll get even with you."

Trying to wish away these bad people or trying to invent additional other cheeks to turn is a good bit like facing a king cobra 3 feet from your face and hoping, if

3

you smile, it will decide to take up needlepoint. Ms. Anonymous's motto for bad guys is "nuke 'em 'til they glow!" That's the credo, kiddo.

That's not innocent cynicism, folks, nor is it irony. It's true. So what is the difference between an innocent and me? For starters, I don't wonder where all of the mall Santas go after December 25.

Although I've been called a dangerous criminal by the grown-ups in the law enforcement racket, one person's criminal could be another person's freedom fighter. Remember Vietnam? Besides, one of the perks of being a criminal is the major abundance of fun personal freedoms, i.e., you do what you want to when you want to, etc.

One of those etc.'s is being able to get back at the evil folks and institutions who give you all of the heartache and trouble. I refer, of course, to "marks." And, as I've preached since the beginning of these screeds, you always first try to solve the problem peacefully, with civility and with proper lotus-eater sensitivity.

After your patient attempts to settle things in a civil manner fail and you are met with more hostility, it's time to move along. Rarely do these mark 'n you matters work out well, though Orrin Sackett does tell a story of a peaceful fella about 6 1/2 feet tall who was challenged to a duel by a hothead who was a tad over 5 feet tall. The big man didn't want to fight, so he accepted the challenge and, as is the custom, had the choice of weapons. He chose sledgehammers in 6 feet of water. The thought made the hothead laugh, the challenge was withdrawn, and the two became the best of friends.

Apocryphal or not, it's a great story, and it makes my point. But, more likely you're going to have to meet that mark's bullying challenge. Orrin's story? Personally, I think he made it up.

There are a lot of marks out there, and dealing with them is not fun. It's like trying to fornicate with a porcupine; it's your one prick against a hundred of 'em. The idea, you see, is to make the mark feel as if he were shitting exploding shotgun shells, metaphorically speaking.

If your resolve to read further is beginning to melt, please go immediately to the chapter titled MARKS. Read it now.

Remember, your mark is not a victim; he or she is your enemy. Your mark is the poster person for greed, crudity, or stupidity. A mark is someone who sticks it so far up a real victim's ass that the victim's ears wiggle.

As Tell Sackett, Orrin's brother, once said, "I hadn't baited no hook, yet this gent (a mark!) won't stop bobbin' my cork."

Play "El DeGuello" and give that asshole no quarter.

And, speaking of assholes, that reminds me of one of my former co-workers, a nasty lesbian named Bobbi. One day she was fussing around worrying about what to wear to a Halloween party sponsored by her Single Losers Supporthose Group. I told her it would be most fitting if she would smear peanut butter around her mouth and go as an asshole.

Ahhh yes, uneasy is the head that wears the toilet seat.

As you peruse this book of humor, remember Hayduke's Prayer: "Grant me patience, O Lord, but please hurry! Thus, blessed are we who can laugh at ourselves, for we shall never cease to be amused."

"The printer . . . without him, tyrants and humbugs in all countries would have their own way."
—Charles Dickens

GENERAL ADVICE

Throughout this book, I make universal reference to the "mark," which is a street label hung on the victim—male or female—of a scam, con, or act of vengeance. In our case, the mark is a bully—anyone or anything—who has done something unpleasant, foul, or unforgivable to you, your family, your property, or your friends. Never think of a mark as the victim of dirty tricks. Think of the mark as a very deserving bully, a target of your revenge.

Before you study any of the specific sections of this book, read these vital paragraphs. They tell you how to prepare before going into action.

1. *Prepare a plan.* Plan all details before you take action at all. Don't even ad-lib something from this book without an exact plan of what you're going to do and how. If your campaign involves a series of actions, make a chronological chart (don't forget to destroy it when you're through) and then coordinate your efforts. Make a list of possible problems. Plan

what you'll do if you get caught—depending upon who catches you. You must have every option, contingency, action, reaction, and evaluation planned in advance. Remember, time is usually on the side of the trickster. As Winston Churchill, one of my favorite heroes for many, many reasons, once said, "A lie gets halfway around the world before the truth gets in its boots." Or, as that old Sicilian homily goes, "Revenge is a dish best served cold," which means don't strike while your ire is hot. Wait. Plan. Think. Learn.

2. *Gather intelligence*. Do what a real intelligence operative would do: compile a file on your mark. How detailed and thorough you are depends upon your mark. For a simple get-even number, you obviously need less inside information than if you're planning an involved, time-release campaign. Before you start spying, make a written list of all the important things you need to know about that target—be it a person, company, or institution.

3. *Buy away from home*. Any supplies, materials, or services you need must be purchased away from where you live. Buy far in advance and pay in cash. Try to be as inconspicuous and colorless as possible. Don't talk unnecessarily with people. The best rule here is the spy's favorite: a good operative will get lost in a crowd of one. The idea is for people not to remember you.

4. *Never tip your hand*. Don't get cocky, cute 'n clever and start dropping hints about who's doing what to whom. I know that may sound stupid, but some would-be tricksters are gabby. Of course, in some

7

cases, this will not apply, e.g., unselling car customers at the dealership or other tricks in which the scenario demands your personal involvement.

5. ***Try to make your punishment fit the crime***. Just as in Sir William Gilbert's poem, which Sir Arthur Sullivan set to music and called *The Mikado*, your punishment should fit your mark's crime. One benefit is that the irony may not be wasted on the mark. Another is the humor you will realize. After all, it's the same old biblical eye-and-tooth stuff.

6. ***Never admit anything***. If accused, act shocked, hurt, outraged, or amused, whichever seems appropriate. Deny everything, unless, again, your plan involves overt personal involvement. If you're working covertly, stay that way. The only cool guy out of Watergate was G. Gordon Liddy, who kept his mouth shut.

7. ***Never apologize; it's a sign of weakness. Besides, they can't prove anything***. Normally, harassment of a citizen is a low-priority case with the police. The priority increases along with the mark's socioeconomic status in the community and his or her political connections. If you are at war with a corporation, utility, or institution, that's a different ball game. They often employ private security people, sometimes retired federal or state investigators. By habit, these people may not play according to the law. If you play dirty tricks upon a government body, prepare to have a case opened. But how hard it is pursued depends upon a lot of factors. Understanding all this ahead of time is part of your intelligence planning before you get started.

THE ELEVEN COMMANDMENTS OF REVENGE

Thanks to my Apostle of Revenge, Dick Smegma, I humbly present for your perusal, belief, and adherence the Eleven Commandments of Revenge. Stay faithful to them and you'll enjoy a lot of yucks without suffering the heartbreak of being caught.

1. ***Thou shalt neither trust nor confide in anyone!*** If you do, that person could eventually betray you. Even if it is a relative or spouse, don't tell anybody what you are up to. Implicated accomplices are OK.

2. ***Thou shalt never use thy own telephone for revenge business!*** Always use a public telephone or that of an unwitting mark so calls cannot be traced back to you or to someone who knows you.

3. ***Thou shalt not touch revenge documents with thy bare hands!*** Bare hands leave fingerprints. Wear gloves.

4. ***Thou shalt become a garbage collector!*** Once your victim places his trash outside his home or office for pickup, it is legal for you to pick it up yourself. You can learn a lot about your mark by sifting through his papers and such. The pros do it all the time.

5. ***Thou shalt bide thy time before activating a revenge plot!*** Give the victim time to forget about you and what he's done to wrong you. Getting even too soon makes it easier for him to discover who's doing it.

6. ***Thou shalt secure a "mail drop" address in another city!*** You don't want revenge mail being traced back to your residence/home, do you?

7. ***Thou shalt learn everything there is to know about thy victim!*** The best revenge schemes or plans are hatched by people who know their victims better than their victims know themselves.

8. ***Thou shalt pay cash all the time in a revenge plot!*** Checks, money orders, and other paper transfers can be traced back to you. Cash cannot.

9. ***Thou shalt trade with merchants who have never heard of you!*** Do business with people only once when involved in a revenge plot. You can wear a disguise so the people you are involved with will have trouble identifying you in a legal confrontation.

10. ***Thou shalt never threaten thy victim!*** Why warn your intended victim that you are going to get even? When bad things begin to happen to your victim—whether or not you caused them—your vic-

tim will remember your threat, and he or she will set out to even the score with you.

11. ***Thou shalt not leave evidence lying around, however circumstantial!*** If you are thought to be actively engaged in having fun at your mark's expense, the authorities may visit you. Thus, it would be prudent not to have any of my books at home or in the office. Note well what Francois de La Rochefoucauld wrote in *Maximes*, "The height of cleverness is to be able to conceal it."

HOW TO
USE THIS BOOK

I have arranged these subjects by method and mark, listing them alphabetically. In addition to using the obvious subject headings, you can also do a cross-reference of your own. Or you can adapt a method listed for one mark to another mark or situation. This book is as versatile as your own imagination.

While this mix 'n' match versatility is standard, the personalized nasty touch is still the best. Another effective part of this business is the anticipation of further damage after your initial attack. This is grand psychological warfare.

This entire concept reminds me of what Ralph Waldo Emerson wrote about a weed, "And what is a weed? It's a plant whose virtues have not yet been discovered."

However, the real use of this book is vicarious humor. You don't actually do these stunts, just read about them and laugh.

CAUTION

The schemes, tricks, scams, stunts, cons, and scenarios presented here are for information and amusement purposes only. It is not my intent that you use this book as a manual or trickster's cookbook. I certainly don't expect that anyone who reads this book would actually ever do any of the things described here. This book is written solely to entertain and inform my readers, not to instruct or persuade anyone to commit any unpleasant or illegal act. Given my own mild disposition, I could hardly tell someone else to make any of these tactics operational.

Consider the case of mistaken vengeance that took place in Vienna, Austria, in 1985, when Leopold Renner thought his wife was cheating on him because he saw her holding hands with another man. The shocked husband stuffed 27 of her live, exotic pets—one after another—into the churning garbage disposal. Down went screaming parakeets, hamsters, mice, and tarsiers into a gushy gruel feeding into the sewage drains.

Fact: His wife, Frieda, had been holding the hand of

13

her brother, whom she had not seen in a dozen years, and she was bringing him home to meet her husband. True story.

A good Hayduker works smart and covers all of the angles. Plan for all options and all contingencies. And remember this worthy advice from J.R.R. Tolkien, "It doesn't do to leave a live dragon out of your calculations if you live near him."

If you're going to kick over an anthill, do it fast and right the first time and don't get your boot stuck, or the ants will eat you alive. Ahh, that's meant as an analogy, of course. Likewise, you don't go hunting vampires without making certain you have garlic, a cross, plus wooden stakes and a mallet.

Yes, caution is important. Don't take a foolish or stupid mark lightly. Personally, dangerous fools frighten me more than clever enemies. Remember that old Shinto proverb that a nest of vipers is not as deadly as one hungry man.

Finally, some readers will be outraged by my attitudes, language, and view of our systems, people, and institutions. I do not see our world through the same rose-colored glasses that they do. My glasses are jaundice-colored. If my language, ideas, and philosophies offend you, remember, gentle reader, that vulgarity is the garlic in the salad of taste.

MARK

As in my other books, I use the word *mark* to refer to the object of your revenge. A mark can be a person, institution, company, animal, object—just about anything that has hurt you in any manner or continues to do so. Usually, you've tried all of the ethical, legal, moral, and Golden Rule things to make everyone happy. You're a paragon of patience, a vigor of virtue. But your mark is a true anus stain and won't stop bullying, annoying, or bothering you.

This is when you begin to get angry. You're getting so frustrated and angry that you want to watch a rabid moray eel eat the mark's eyeballs—while the mark is still alive. Or you feel as if your mark needs to be in the nearest intensive-care unit.

Hold those thoughts, because that's when it's time to call on George Hayduke, bullybuster. Within the pages of this book, you'll discover all sorts of bullybusting ideas, ranging from the mildly sardonic to the bombastically devastating.

But, as a matter of early warning intelligence, how

can you spot a potential mark? Thanks to some exhaustive research at the Hayduke Institute of Semiological Research, Dr. Bruno McManmon, project director, has come up with some characteristics that fit a computer-generated model to profile myriad marks. This profile indicates that a potential mark:

- thinks that when she/he defecates, the odor of lilacs fills the stalls;
- is the sort of person for whom it would be redundant to claim ignorance;
- often carries that rotten-guilty look, like a nasty little boy who's peed his pants;
- has all of the sexual appeal of rancid lard;
- has a foul personality that stands out like a neon cockroach in a bowl of grits;
- blows dead bears for a quarter and gives change;
- would sell his/her grandmother to a Nigerian brothel if the price were right;
- has the personality of week-old sinus drainage;
- has the ethical standards of a Bolivian drug dealer selling poisoned heroin to kids in your neighborhood.

I could go on, but I suspect you get the drift. A mark is someone you want to come down on to make your neighborhood a nicer place to live. Nothing wrong with that.

Remember, for your mark, your revenge has to be his or her season in hell. Consider *Hamlet*, Act II, Scene 2, "O God, I could be bounded in a nutshell and count myself a king of infinite space, were it not that I have bad dreams." You want your mark to have bad dreams, especially those dreams that end with: *it could happen again, asshole!*

Marks are all around us, although there are statistically few of them when compared to the nice folk. It's your choice whether to respond to or ignore your mark. As the offended, you must choose whom to fricassee on the hot coals of their ill-chosen act or words. So, to all of the marks in your life, I offer a curse from an old shaman I knew in another life in a dark, evil section of a small island south of the United States:

> *"The death fart from a terrified adult is a thousand times worse than anything a live body can emit. May such a death fart multiply a thousand times in the nostrils of your enemy "*

> —Moloch Beelzebub
> Hinchazon Cay, 1980

ABORTION

It's been my experience that many pro-lifers are intellectually inbred religious runts who insist that life begins at conception. Next, they'll insist that life begins at inception. That could create all sorts of interesting scenarios.

For example, it would lower every kid's drinking age by nine months. Or, if your sweetie refuses to have sex with you, is that an argument for pro-life or pro-choice? Perhaps, Rasputin can offer some insight.

After trying to rationally counsel couples on all options in the abortion issue, Rasputin has come to the conclusion that many of the most rabid pro-life activists are themselves walking, talking arguments for retroactive abortion. Our good and devoted counselor played a little prank on them. "I learned that my community required a permit to parade and picket. So, I called the activist leader of our local pro-life group and told him there was going to be a big pro-choice demonstration, giving him the time and place. I told the guy that the pro-choice folks had a permit and that I, an irate city employee, was devastated . . . would he do something?"

Rasputin continues, "Obviously, there was no demonstration when the pro-lifers arrived with their signs and counterdemonstration. Naturally, I had called the local police to report an illegal rally."

In a follow-up, Rasputin and his pal Biggus located a used copy of *The Satanic Bible*, put a "Book Property of . . ." label inside the cover, inscribed the name of the local pro-life leader, and left the tome in a pew at the local Very Fundamental Church of Tiny Minds and Loud Braying Asses.

The Vindictive Female reports another tactic used by pro-choice folks. It's called Adopt a Picket and it goes like this. Whenever there is an antiabortion demonstration, you take a photo of each demonstrator. Each photo is given to a pro-choice person who's agreed in advance to make a small monetary donation to the local pro-choice cause in that photo subject's name, and to contact that pro-lifer to offer counseling, humor, advice, old leftovers, and other charitable acts.

Ms. Vindictive Female told me that she and some friends "adopted" her boss' ugly wife because of her obnoxious support of violent antiabortion protest, e.g., firebombings and ax handles.

"We sent her a letter saying that $100 had been donated in her name to Planned Parenthood and another $100 to Abortion Referral Services (a local clinic). We thanked her for her generous support and told her that we planned to make the public aware of her generosity and belief in free choice. We signed the letter with some illegible name," Ms. Vindictive Female says with a laugh.

Rev. Milhouse Pakalolo, grand rectum of the Quayle Family Values Foundation, once wrote, "We feel that a rape or incest-enhanced little breeder must carry her child to term. There's nothing like a baby to bring a gal and her daddy closer."

19

Here's my question. If that dad gets convicted of rape, is sent to prison, then paroled, can he, as father, sue for visitation rights? Just asking.

ADDITIVES

I first met Dollar Bill Vincent in the gorgeous state of Kentucky in 1960, and we've stayed close friends, which perhaps says more for both of us than either of us. Dollar Bill once told me that "the body's greatest poison is in the mind." While my friend may have been correct, his words of wisdom are not inclusive on the subject of either poisons or additives. Of course, it might have been the nature of the work he and I were engaged in at the time, too. Let us consider the words of others. For example, as a generous practitioner, Mr. Eighth Wonder of the World suggests, "George, you can concoct your own painful potions right at home. Try pricking some prick of a mark with this.

"Mix Tabasco sauce and strong toothpaste together and make sure the mark introduces it, or has it introduced, into some sensitive portion of the anatomy, like a cut," Mr. World suggests.

Going up the scale of discomfort, though, Matt the Lizard and Apple Cori found some research that says right-handed males are statistically more susceptible to

Alzheimer's disease than folks who are left-handed. Further, Ms. Cori learned that aluminum poisoning features strongly in Alzheimer history.

Our dear scientist thought about adding aluminum sulfate to the punch given to freeloading drunks. She says the additive dries out the mouth, thus making folks even more likely to drink, and, well, you get the picture.

Picture? What picture? What were we discussing?

Actually, there are some positive things about Alzheimer's disease. For instance, you meet new people everyday, some of them several times. And, you can hide your own Easter eggs.

In past books I have suggested various delivery systems for additives. The Ruthless Gangster tells me that I should have included hair spray bottles.

"They're translucent at best, so the mark cannot see what's lurking inside. You could fill the mark's bottle with urine, diluted blood, runny diarrhea, skunk scent, oil . . . the combinations are endless."

Speaking of delivery systems, Jake the Ox shares the thought that bottle cappers, used by home brewers, can also be used as bottle recappers after something has been added to the mark's bottle's original contents.

Two very good old boys who are also two loyal friends have come up with homespun remedies for deserving marks. First, my large pal from Florida, one of the bravest men I know, told me about food thieves stealing lunches from workers in a plant. Ken told me that instead of using OTC Ex-Lax, he easily obtained from a pharmacist some yellow phenolphtalein crystals. This is the active ingredient in most laxatives.

"We sprinkled these lightly on targeted lunches, and, sure enough, the villains stole them. As the crystals are very light, almost colorless, each thief never saw a thing and chowed down. Next day the two culprits were taken to a local hospital with explosive lower GI problems.

"They were back at work two days later, and nobody said a word. No more lunches were taken, though."

Speaking of health care, I recall Dr. Death's treatment of Horrible Night Nurse Cheryl who was mean and miserable to all. She used to order student nurses to bring her fresh-squeezed orange juice at all hours despite their other work. Dr. Death added a generous dollop of postassium citrate to her juice. The taste was bitter, but she dutifully drank it with Dr. Death's urging.

"For the next two shifts, Nasty Nursey was too preoccupied with being perched on the porcelain throne to be mean to others," Dr. Death relates.

Ray Heffer from Kansas City says it's cheaper, easier, and more fun to make your own itching powder than to buy it from novelty stores.

"Better yet, yours will be lots more effective and stronger than the wimpy stuff they sell. Here's what you do. Pick up some clumps of hair cuttings next time you're at the barber shop. Take 'em home and mix them in a container of liquid laundry bleach. Let this soak for a couple of hours. Spread the hair out and let it dry. Then, shred it up real fine with scissors or in a blender.

"To use, just sprinkle it lightly on bedding, clothes, or directly on your mark, be it human or otherwise. The stuff really makes a big-time itch, and the only way to get rid of it is a strong shower with lots of soap. The mark also has to wash all of the material contacted, too."

George from Guam wrote to share with us a fine product called Visible Detection Paste, which is available from most police supply shops. When this stuff contacts human skin, it turns the contact areas a bright purple. It's very tough to wash off. George suggested useful applications on door knobs, armrests, chairs, toilet seats. I bet you can think of many other useful applications

While in the mythical Latinland resort, Paladinista, my splendid amigo Guillermo had the good fortune to be vacationing with several Evian-guzzling freeloaders who relied on good old Guillermo to freely replenish the hoard of food and drink they consumed.

Health freaks to a persyn, they freaked in paranoid fear of the local tap water, fearing even to bathe in it. Thus they let Guillermo buy their Evian for them, good guy that he is. Soon tiring of being the public budget, Guillermo waited until his Yuppie tourists went to the golf course. Then, instead of buying new water for them, he simply refilled their empty Evian bottles   with the local tap water.

Finally, since most marks are assholes, we'll close with this from the Madhitter, who asks, "Ever replace the contents of someone's hemorrhoid cream with Vicks Vapo Rub?"

Now there is some sphincter twitching time.

ADVERTISING

Some years ago, my old army buddy Bill Jackson gave up the outlaw life to become a newspaper publisher. One of the deep secrets of our misspent youth is that we also once worked together for the same advertising agency. We were good ad men, Bill and I. Even on a bad day we could talk a hungry cat down off a fish wagon. I explain all of this so that you'll trust my credibility when I write about advertising and revenge, as the two go together like flies and shit.

Business cards are an effective form of advertising. Naomi has an interesting idea for your mark's business cards. Print some especially nasty ones on behalf of your mark, your mark's business, etc. You can be as PG-13 or XXX as you wish with your message. The second shoe to drop, then, is to take the bogus cards to the most mark-inappropriate locales to dispense them.

A local business played head games with The Krazed Kaliko from Koko Head, a very bad move, sort of like french kissing a wasp nest. Kaliko had a friend in another state print 5,000 very colorful and professional-looking fliers advertising that folks NOT patronize the aforementioned business.

Kaliko adds, "I really made them look like their usual ads, except that I blasted them, insisted that people never shop with 'us.' I wrote it first person, too. I even included a noncoupon that told readers if they'd bring this to our store and NOT shop there, 'we'd' pay them a $10 bonus."

He and several trusted friends put fliers on car windshields in local malls, plus handed them out on a college campus. Kaliko says the offending shop was swamped by irate noncustomers the next day, and the police had to be called to break up the unpleasantness. He notes, too, that the shop ran a series of radio spots telling people not to come to their shop, that the flier was bogus.

Usually, old pal Biggus has truly fun stuff. This time, he offers some big nasty. He suggests a classified advertisement under the "legal announcement" section of your local newspaper.

"You need to do this with style, e.g., create some professional-looking letterhead from a district justice and have someone dressed very professionally bring it to the paper," Biggus says.

This stunt works well with smaller newspapers whose staff is more likely to buy your con without question. Now, here's what the ad says:

TO: (mark's name and address). This is to inform you under State (name one) statute that you have been charged with violation of Sec. 1204.243-J of the (state) criminal penal code. The above is a felony of the second class involving (list specific charges here, like statutory rape, child molestation, arson, buggering a sheep or a corpse, or whatever). You are hereby directed to surrender yourself to the nearest law enforcement facility, accompanied by your attorney.

Biggus says this one played very well in Idaho, Texas, Oklahoma, plus a few other venues where he has used this type of ad to get back at some bully.

Remember when Cabbage Patch dolls were being bootlegged, hijacked, and sold for $200 each? Are they even on the market today? Steve Bauer has found a way to make this human greed pay off.

Steve says to pick the hot item of the minute that everyone is looking to buy. Take out an advertisement for your mark telling folks that he has unlimited quantities of the item. Make his/her price somewhat less than current market value. Be sure you put your mark's name and home phone in the ad, too.

Tector Gorch told me about an antibillboard guy named Jan who was campaigning against my least favorite form of visual pollution, i.e., billboards. "Old Monkeywrenchers used to cut them down with chainsaws. But, after a large board fell on top of Guy Mills, Lyle, Tector, Freddie, and I stopped that.

"Instead, we are into creative, independent billboarding. I figured that since we can't beat the Asshole Chamberpot of Commerce Dweebs, we could help them. So, we've been putting up our own cleverly designed artwork over theirs. For instance, we have a community service ad promoting safe sex by showing a well-drawn young couple engaging in mutual masturbation. Another of our graphically illustrated public service billboard advocates vomiting into toilets and not onto the floor. We also promote recycled sanitary napkins and booger soup.

"Our billboard sheets, done by like-thinking volunteer artists, are simply pasted over offending commercial ones."

Finally, Sandy Zaft Pakalolo was disgusted by a local shop in her mall that constantly runs bait 'n switch advertising without fear of local prosecution, as the judge's wife owns the place.

"With the help of a printer who hated them, too, I was able to duplicate the shop's logo and style on a bunch of discount coupons which I had some kiddies hand out at the mall entrance. I also made sure stacks of the coupons were placed in local supermarkets and, which was funny to me, in her two competitors' stores," Sandy related with mirth.

Bill Jackson and I used to call advertising "the business of giving the public the business."

AIRLINES

I just read that the Federal Aviation Administration has responded to concerns over passenger health by banning airlines from serving meals. Actually, WarHawk says that delays and late arrivals are far more damaging than mere food poisoning. I agree.

WarHawk gets bored by airline delays, so in a gentle way of amusing himself he likes to go to the white paging telephone and have the unsuspecting airlines page various nonexistent friends for him. Some examples include Dr. Harry P. Ness, Rocky Piles, Philip Mabutt, Hannibal Lecter, Seymour Hennie, et. al. The secret is to spell, not say the names, to the operator.

An unwilling but frequent business flier, Captain Prickman has had more than his share of luggage lost, spindled, and mutilated. The experience gave him an amusing way to get even.

"I visit yard and rummage sales to buy very cheap luggage. Then I get some classy-looking tags to fill out with my mark's name/address/home phone, plus a strongly worded reward offer of $25 for safe return of 'my' suitcase," the good Captain relates.

His next step is to plant these bogus bombs in the airport area, but also near nuisance bars, flophouse hotels, whorehouses, etc. Soon, your mark will have all sorts of folks returning lost luggage and anxious for the "reward."

This next stunt was told to me as an entertaining story by The Scuzzbuster, a licensed private investigator. It is a truly nasty story, but as Scuzzbuster's mark is the coverboy for the Guiness Book of World's Rectums, I offer it for your amusement.

Scuzzbuster learned that his mark was going to be in Florida the same week that a serial killer was to be executed. First, Scuzzbuster got a certified copy of the mark's birth certificate and used this to get a state identification card. This ID card had Scuzzbuster's photo with the mark's name and address. He used this to buy a handgun in the mark's name.

"I got one of those military-style pistols that looks like a machine pistol, thinking of the visual impact. Next, I clipped several newspaper stories about the condemned killer and taped them to a single sheet of paper upon which I had typed demands that unless the killer was freed, 'I' (the mark) would execute people on the aircraft," Scuzzbuster explained.

He carefully wrapped the unloaded handgun in with the papers and put it all in a small shaving gear case embossed with the mark's initials. A little surveillance told Scuzzbuster that the mark packed his car for the Florida trip the night before departure.

"I came back to his place at 3 A.M. and got into the asshole's car easily. I put my 'gift' into his carry-on bag and left. I wish I could have been at the airport when the X-rays picked up the handgun. But, you and I know the rules," Scuzzbuster said with a sigh.

He did say that he heard all about the arrest on the local radio station's news and added that the regional TV station covered the story, too. Local, state, and federal officials were not buying the mark's frantic claims that he was a victim of a setup. This didn't wash well because according to the *official records*, the gun was his and had been purchased directly by him. The result was a stiff fine, a suspended federal prison sentence, and several years' probation.

Scuzzbuster told me that he really didn't do this, he just thought about it. Of course, I believed him.

In another criminal development, Biggus Piraphicus thought of an evil way to pay back a mark. If you know your mark's airline reservation information, you call the airline office directly at the airport. You identify yourself as a law enforcement official and tell the airline person that Mark is a fugitive from justice and that you have agents on their way to the airport to arrest him. Tell the airline person that the mark is an armed sociopath and very dangerous.

The airline person will no doubt alert security. The results could be amusing. Naturally you would not want to do this for real, as impersonating a law enforcement official is a serious crime, which makes you wonder why more of ours aren't in jail.

Penelope Puss used to be a flight attendant and had to work with a very disagreeable person whom we'll call Mark. I won't detail Mark's evil ways, but he deserved Penelope's fun.

"My favorite trick was during preflight talk to the passengers. I broke open two ammonia vials and placed them in the dummy oxygen mask that Mark was going to demonstrate. He couldn't stop coughing. It was wild and fun," she related.

And, for a final bit of advice, we turn to Dingboo Hassam, manager of several convenience stores in Pukeboro, Utah. Dingboo says to be very careful about long-term parking lots in your regional airport.

"Mob guys have made long-term parking their cemetery of choice for disposing of personnel problems. You could come home to find strange people in the trunk of your car," says Dingboo.

Speaking of finding lost baggage, I think I'll excuse myself now and go tether my blimp.

ANIMALS

Julie Jay's dog, Jimmy, drives her to strong drink. Just the other day she yelled at him for peeing on her carpet. Of course, Jimmy couldn't point out to her that she does the same thing in his water bowl, which is part of her bathroom.

And, speaking of literate humanists, Steve Wilson has a harmless variation of the fish-eating stunt I suggested in an earlier book. Rather than mess up a perfectly innocent goldfish, Steve suggests that you do the same stunt and use a sliver of carrot, instead.

Recall, you want to impress, horrify, or whatever someone, so you reach into an aquarium, pull out a live goldfish and swallow it. Instead, Steve says to hide a sliver of carrot in your paw and when you reach for the fish, flash the carrot instead, then eat it.

Same impact, yet you saved a fish's life. Was it Wanda?

Ray Heffer likes rats. He says if you're having problems with a neighbor or someone who owns a warehouse, business, school, or whatever, Heffer thinks that rats make the perfect tenant.

"Buy rats from a medical supply house. Be sure you get both male and female versions," Heffer advises. "Turn them loose in your mark's building with a good supply of water, wheat, corn, etc. Rats breed more progeny than Third World citizens and are generally a lot more destructive."

Master Zimmerman likes to meet animals after they're dead so he can either nail them to or hang them from his mark's front door, business, or home. Being an environmentally good citizen, Brother Zimmerman sees this as an excellent way to recycle fresh roadkill.

While people could get arrested for Hayduking, birds seldom are arrested, tried, or issued sentences for anything. That's why the Birdman of Anarchy likes to feature birds in his fun.

"Seagulls are true scavengers; they'll eat anything. They have a 30 minute digestive system that's very regular. They also flock to feed. Does that give you any ideas?" the Birdman asks us.

I am sure the semidiscerning reader can already picture someone littering a mark's car with bread crumbs. Or, as the old Erie fisherman, John Young, a friend I really dig, told me, sardine or other strong fish oil will also attract gulls without all the visual litter of bread crumbs. He says it brings 'em in swarms, and that the end result, you should pardon his pun, is the same. The Prairie Dog also endorses this option, saying that gulls will circle for hours searching for the source of the fishy odor, all the while recycling their meals.

Dirty Dan is another socially correct person. When he walks his dog he carries a supply of Baggies so he can dispose of his dog's dumpings properly. Some of Dan's neighbors aren't so nice. One has loud parties which bother Dan and the other neighbors. Another uses their quiet residential street like the Bonneville Salt Flats.

"On those occasions when our neighbors are impolite and when my Fido's relief is still warm, soft, and fresh in my Baggies, I deposit a generous and representative sample on the driver's side door handles of the appropriate vehicles."

Savage Henry is another good neighbor. He says to pick up all of the dead animals in your neighborhood—the rats, cats, squirrels, bunnies, etc. Put each in a bag and keep them in your freezer until you have 20 to 30 of them.

"These frozen little creatures make wonderful lawn ornaments for some deserving neighbor. Or place them on lawn furniture or near the patio or pool. But they should be visible to the other neighbors. Sometimes I couple them in sexually explicit positions before freezing," says Henry.

Obviously, a good case of letting your hare down.

Alabama's Terminator X dealt with a unruly roadhog, one of those cretins who drives a pumped-up pickup that you need a 21-foot ladder to enter. Terminator X found a previously alive and very bloated raccoon corpse. He tied it to the back bumper of his mark's truck and stuffed the gross carcass underneath.

"Despite this asshole's truck being suspended way above his wheels he never looked, just jumped in and roared away. Soon, one of Alabama's law officers had him offside the road trying to explain why he was towing a dead 'coon behind his truck. This good ole boy ain't hardly as literate as the 'coon, even in its dead state," Terminator says with a laugh.

One of Jon Moyer's chemistry teachers told him about a nasty dog that kept dumping garbage cans and spreading debris. The teacher laced a hamburger patty with 1 ounce of antimony. The dog ate it and within a week had lost all of its hair for nearly a month. Jon says this will work with humans, too.

Bill Dyer passes along some humor, too. Bill says to allow some dog urine to dry in a pan. Reconstitute it with alcohol, then place in a small bottle, e.g., a nasal spray container. Spray the contents on the pant legs or hemline of your mark's clothing.

The alcohol dries quickly and leaves the residue of dog urine. Other dogs that get close will probably try to mark the mark by leaving their own calling card on the clothing, too.

On the other paw, if the dog does happen to fall in love with the mark's leg, perhaps you should have the decency to leave them alone for a few moments.

Speaking of dogs, Jim Neumiller tells me that those ultrasonic dog training whistles, the ones we can't hear, also have a positive effect on untrained dogs, too. It makes them bark.

Jim says this gives you the power to decide when that nasty neighbor's dog will start in on the big-time noisy barking act. You can use this information a little or a lot, Jim says, depending upon your resolve, mission, and goal.

I guess the idea of all of this animal humor is to make you stand out from the otters.

ANSWERING MACHINES

Televelocity is a new word found in the *Feinman's Dictionary of Technology*. It is defined as the speed at which one tries to reach the telephone before your answering machine kicks on.

At one time, Prairie Dog worked with an especially nasty man whose one-boss business depended heavily on an answering machine. Hence, as Prairie Dog explained, "If he lived by his machine, I was going to help him die by it, figuratively speaking, of course."

Of course.

Prairie Dog called and left the following message. "Hello, Mr. (mark's name)? This is Dr. Bollocks at the (local) County Health Department. We've treated a young lady this week for a venereal disease and, according to law, she must list her sexual partners. As she told us you were one of her regulars, we must insist that you come in for immediate examination and that you cease all sexual contact."

The kicker here is that the mark had a very jealous live-in gal pal who acted as both unofficial secretary for

the answering machine and as very official jealous keep-
er of his morals.

This one was a lose/lose situation for all but Prairie
Dog, of course, who enjoyed it all the way.

Dick Smegma is, as usual, skating around the rim of
legality in his humor. But, as this is strictly hypothetical,
you'll enjoy his story.

Dick says to change the *outgoing* message on your
mark's machine when you know s/he will be gone for a
good while. You change the message to say, "Hello, operator, this is (mark's name and phone number). If this
is a collect call from area code XXX, the charges are accepted. To the calling party, please leave your message
at the sound of the beep. Thank you."

Of course, you use your calling area code for the
XXX listed above. Then, you and/or confederates call
the number and leave enough bullshit messages to fill
the message tape. At this point, Dick says you have three
options. One, you can either call and retrieve the messages, erase them, and start all over again. Or you can
record a new outgoing message with groans or screams
or satanic chants or whatever. Or you can simply record
"blank" as an outgoing message.

Dick's point is to pick the highest rate times to make
your calls. The mark returns and has a huge telephone
bill with almost no explanation, especially if you've
erased the outgoing evidence. As always, Dick is telling
you this just for laughs, with no other intent.

My dear friend, The Reverend Doktor McGeary of St.
Onan's Church of the Helping Hand, always includes a
little sermon on his outgoing tape messages. Last time I
called he was giving some very touching readings from
Leviticus 20:15

Most answering machine jollies involve outgoing

messages, as we've just seen. Biggus insists that the incoming message should fight back. Personally, I was always more concerned about incoming than outgoing. But, let's see what Biggus has cranked up here.

If you know your mark is expecting an important call for the answering machine, it might be well to help out by putting a fresh tape on the machine's incoming side. Biggus suggests a tape that is permanently blank or has white noise on it, or one of nursery rhymes, or else one of candid sexual noises.

Hey, don't frown at me; I don't own a telephone.

AUTOS

What do you call a Far Eastern monk who sells reincarnations? What else, a used karma dealer.

OK, so what we're dealing with in this section are mouth-breathing marks whose IQs are less than the gear ratio of their rides and whose carburetors you'd like to throttle.

The aptly named Psycho once had a nasty mark molest a mutually known lady friend after lying to get her to take a brief, innocent drive. It was shocking behavior, and Psycho responded in kind to help his friend.

"I attached the stripped end of a thin wire to the spark plug boot, then ran it through the firewall, under the floor mat and front seat, to the back of that seat. I stripped the other end's insulation and laid bare wire out on the seat. I did this at night when the jerk was in a bar," Psycho reports.

The deal works when the mark sits down on that bare wire and cranks over the car's motor. We're talking about upwards of 70,000 volts but no amps; sorry, you won't fry the guy. Psycho's friends, who'd gone drinking with the mark to witness the fun, said the guy lost control of his body functions and pissed himself when the power hit him.

Speaking of pricks, Penisdrip had a sports car that he adored. He also liked to roar up to crosswalks and frighten pedestrians by stopping 2 feet from them. After repeated pleas from neighbors to stop this dangerous behavior went ignored, Doc Byte took action.

"I took a length of black, insulated wire and looped in about 20 black thumbtacks. Then I put the entire assembly around his windshield wiper. I did this on a rainy, dark day while he was at work. Now, Penisdrip has a very badly marred windshield on his expensive car," Doc explains.

Sometimes, the price of learning manners is expensive.

Do you know a driver whose rule of the road is that the vehicle with the biggest tires always has the right of way? Talking Back from Georgia tired of that and decided to act.

"Like a SWAT team, my friends and I located the offending vehicles and removed the balancing weights from selected wheels. Some were remounted 180 degrees out of phase, others just left off," says Talking Back from Georgia.

He said that in extreme cases they'd also add and subtract air from really nasty violators' tires. All of the above greatly decreases tire life.

DRS brought some farm aid to a similar problem by liberating a 5-pound wheel weight from an unused tractor on his uncle's farm. He put this weight on the right front wheel of his mark's car. The result was a shake 'n shimmy that would have made Paula Abdul jealous.

Pyro had an apartment complex neighbor who loved to race into the parking lot, scattering kiddies. Pyro noted that the mark's expensive car's emission control system had an air injection pump feeding through a diverter valve and into the exhaust manifold, as many cars do today. He simply shut down the valve by disabling it, which caused grand damage to the muffler.

"This gets expensive, but even more fun is that sometimes the muffler will 'blow' when the driver decelerates, like the old glasspack mufflers used to burble. Only this time, it really, truly blows . . . even more expensive to repair," he adds.

Considering that used cars come from used car lots, it was easy for Ray Heffer to get back at a crooked dealer who'd done creative readjustment to an odometer and a report of serious alignment damage before selling a car to Ray's friend.

It's illegal to sell rental cars as executive demonstrator cars. Ray managed to obtain some rental agreements specifically completed for several of the autos on this sleazoid dealer's lot. He compiled some gas receipts, travel brochures, and other debris of business travelers. Visiting the lot, Ray secreted a sampling of this rental evidence under seats, in spare tire wells, and other places not likely to be spotted casually.

"I had three options. One was to wait for a real customer to find the planted evidence, another was to 'pretend' to find it myself, or I could make a good-citizen call to the media and to the state attorney general's office," says Heffer.

A more drastic move to cut down on oily operators was suggested by the Chicken Man, who informed me about someone adding valve-grinding compound, aka lapping compound, to the crankcase of his mark's car.

Chicken Man says, "This mark had to have been a truly nasty mutha, because this lapping compound in a car's oil supply will cause the engine to eat itself. I bet he used a fine grit compound and possibly thinned it a bit before he 'changed' the oil for his mark."

Wow, that sure would make a mark grit his teeth, eh?

Slick had an enemy whose pickup truck featured a cap on the bed. Slick procured a length of 1/4-inch steel cable and attached one end to the U-joint on the drive-shaft of his mark's truck. He then looped the cable around the top of the cap and attached the other end to the same U-joint.

"I left a bit of slack in there so the truck could pick up some speed, then, well, you can imagine the sound that followed the cable tightening," Slick related.

Once, a very nasty man purposefully ran over Lonson's dog with his pickup truck. A broken-hearted Lonson related how a true equalizer helped repay the disfavor by pouring two bottles of iodine into the murder vehicle's fuel tank.

Lonson says, "That iodine eventually heats up the pistons so much that when the motor is shut off, or if it seizes up, the pistons and rings are damn near welded to the piston walls."

As usual, grand disciple Dick has nearly out-Smegma'd himself with his chicanery. With all of his intellect and humor, he relates how to have fun with a car and a card.

"Have some business cards printed that duplicate your mark's. Wearing gloves, your accomplice should write on the back of one a note that says, 'SORRY I BUMPED YOUR CAR. PLEASE SEND ME THE REPAIR BILL FOR PROMPT PAYMENT,' then sign as the mark.

"Find your secondary mark's car—the two marks should not know each other, obviously—and be certain there is a small dent or scrape on the street side of the parked vehicle. Put the card under the windshield wiper," says Smegma.

Mark I will be very unhappy with Mark II trying to scam for a mishap that "never happened." Police officers often enjoy these types of cases, or so Russell Bumwad, a Florida PI, told me. He also said that another accomplice could replicate this same trick in several cities across the U.S. to play more with Mark I's mind.

Then, there is that impregnable The Club that absolutely, positively, totally stops car thieves. That's what the ads say, and ads don't lie, do they? Paul Harvey says The Club cuts car theft by 90 percent. Of course, Paul gets paid to say that. Heffer says thieves take less than a minute to beat The Club. Using a hacksaw, they cut the steering wheel in two and remove The Club. Total time: about 45 seconds.

And, as a final piece of advice, offered in good faith by my very own friend and barrister, Attorney Johnson, "Never relieve yourself from a moving vehicle, especially if you're driving at the time."

BANKS

And governments say that guerrilla groups have no sense of humor?

In Santiago, Chile, three folks of the violent persuasion robbed a local Citibank branch of some $10,000 in gringo greenbacks. In return, they left unharmed tellers, plus a plethora of propaganda literature and a dozen condoms. One of the banditos explained that the condoms were for the bank's victims (banks refer to them as customers) so they at least could insist on safety as they were sodomized by the Yankee banks.

I guess it would be fair to ask which is the greater crime, to rob a bank or to own one? The answer brings me to the action of some friends.

Some very close friends have created a corporation known as FTB, Inc., which functions like a bank is supposed to without the usual politics, greed, and plunder. FTB, as a refreshing, healthy change, stands for just what you were thinking, too—Fuck The Bank. True story.

FTB is what the Sedonia Slasher had in mind when the Bored of Directors of the local bank in which he owned stock began making lots of unsecured loans to friends and political bedpanmates, while turning their well-clothed backs on the truly needy and ambitious small business people

The Slasher "leaked" a letter to the director of the regional Federal Reserve office thanking them for "obviously" intervening with the Mark Bank to get him an unsecured loan for his trucking company. The letter was signed by Mark II, a crony of the bank power group players, who promised to direct (wink, wink) extracurricular business to "our" bank.

Obviously, there had been no such loan, but it got the attention of the feds, who sent a curious examiner or two to check on things. According to Slasher, eight months later, most of the bank directors were managing video stores and pumping gas.

The Old Fox is a sly old codger who left the evil city for small-town life. He says, "I like the smaller burgs where the big excitement is a tractor wash or when the traffic light goes on the blink."

Codger to codger, the Old Fox told me, "In one of your books you said folks could write nasty messages on Uncle Sam's money. True, but Uncle doesn't like that."

Old Fox's less-than-risky way to accomplish the same goal is still to write your evil, nasty messages on federal reserve notepaper of the realm, but to circulate these bills by using coin changers. That way the message is still disseminated and your passing risk is gone.

It would take me six pages to detail the hassles that his local bank has caused our loyal Captain Picard. He has tried to make his car payments in a timely fashion, even paying ahead at times. He has given me verbatim exchanges of dialogue between himself and the uncaring clerks.

46

Finally, even Picard had enough. He has taken to strolling up to the remote location drive-in window at his bank on foot and equipped with a box somewhat like the ones inside the remote machine's chute, except that his has the motor set to shoot the contents out, not suck them in.

"Instead of checks, deposits, payments, and other bank documents, I have loaded my box with wasps, fleas, mold spores, fire ants, whatever I choose for that day. I mate my box with their box and let the nasty teller turn on her vacuum device," he adds.

I can hear the WHOOSH from here as Picard's goodies go visit the bank that's caused him so much hassle. Bankers away, maties!

BARS

Way back in 1986, while he was still viable, New York pitbull newspaperman Jimmy Breslin said, "Don't trust that brilliant idea until it survives the hangover." Sometimes a bar gives you one, and other times it's the cretins in the bar.

Such was the experience of Louis Matthews and a friend. The friend got snookered into a game of billiards for money. The bar denizens figured him for a patsy. He won most of their money. So, they physically beat him badly, putting him in the hospital. "No witnesses," of course.

Louis did his recon, developed his plan, then he acted. He and another friend entered the bar and did several fun things. First, they loaded the ashtrays with a mixture of black powder, sugar, and potassium nitrate (saltpeter). When ignited by a lit cigarette, there's a quick, bright flash, followed by a sugar meltdown and a dense cloud of evil-odored smoke.

While this confusion was going on, Louis and friend laced both bathrooms with empty needles, crack vials, and some condoms filled with liquid handsoap. Oh, did I tell you that they'd called the police about a "fire" five minutes earlier?

Louis said that until all of the potential criminal, health, and liability charges were sorted out, the bar was closed for three weeks by the authorities. There's more . . .

While all of that was going on, Louis' friend who got beaten had a sister working in the state insurance regulatory office. A major investigation was opened into the bar's legal liabilities, and the bar owner's insurance company was issued several letters of citation. Of course they were blameless. That's the not the point . . . remember, shit rolls downhill, all the way down, and right in that bar's boarded-up door.

Gay bashers are not my favorite form of roadkill, but what the hell, they leave such greasy skidmarks. Piper Pub found a way to deal with an evil group of regulars in a sports bar whose favorite in-house game was intolerance. At the same time, he managed to make life a lot less fun for a secondary mark, a newspaper editor who'd run an arrogant number on Piper.

"I went to this tough-guy bar on a Friday, and, as I fit in, nobody even looked twice," Piper said. "I got to know the biggest assholes [didja catch his pun?] and their vehicles."

He returned two weeks later and put leaflets under the windshields of these assholes' vehicles. The leaflets advertised that Mr. Secondary Mark, the editor, was beginning a local chapter of the Man/Boy Love Society with regular meetings to be held in this bar. The first organizational meeting was to be on Sunday night.

"I gave the mark's name and home address and told each new member to bring a 12-year-old boy for some real fun of the 'leave your buddy's behind' type."

The police had to be called twice that Sunday, Piper says, by frightened and irate neighbors. The newspaper editor moved to a new city, and the bar is under investigation by the state liquor board.

Less than 10 percent of bartending is serving drinks. The rest is baby-sitting and psychology services. Then you have Mr. Macho hitting on disinterested females. Mark d'Bartender tells a great story.

"Two ladies were being bothered by this scumbag, and he didn't pick up on my discouragement and their attempts to cool him," Mark relates.

The ladies took matters into their own fingers by inviting Mr. Obnoxious to play a new game called "Chi Chi." The one lady told him that the rule was "whatever I do to you, you have to do to my friend."

As you can imagine, Mr. Macho and his Johnson were all tuned to this game. The woman began by running her finger twice on his chin and saying "Chi Chi." Excited, he did the same to her friend. She then stroked her fingers horizontally across his forehead, saying, "Chi Chi." And so on and so on.

What Mr. Macho didn't realize, to the humor of the rest of the bar patrons, was that while Mr. Obnoxious Macho was touching a lady's face, her friend's fingers were loading up from an unclean ashtray. Hence, each time one of the women touched him, she was putting sooty strokes on his face.

BICYCLES

Boris had spent time in Europe, where many people's response to oil dependence is to ride a bicycle. A friend who did bicycle repairs told him about "The Amsterdam Treatment" for rude bicycle folks. Back in the U.S., Boris had occasion to put his memory to practice.

Wanting a bike, he went to a large shop where he was not only mistreated but also cheated. None of the usual turning of all four cheeks did the trick, so Boris decided on Amsterdam.

"I thought about going back to the shop and removing the saddles from as many bicycles as possible, then pouring a bottle of acid-heavy solvent or even a heavy solution of salt paste into the main tube frame, as all are hollow, of course," Boris said.

Rust in peace.

The Sperminator is a graduate of the University of California whose least fond memory of those days is his loser roommate.

"This piece of inconsiderate evil had the personality of a wolverine and was nowhere near as cute. He used everyone else's stuff, ate everyone else's food, broke university furniture and passed the blame off on others . . . a total shit. His only pride was his very expensive mountain bike, which he brought to campus only one time. That was enough," The Sperminator explains.

Even an expensive, complicated mountain bike is very easy to disassemble, needing only a few turns from a few wrenches here and there to disconnect most of the main components. The one time the evil roommate brought his bicycle to campus he made a big mistake.

"He packed it on the luggage rack of his parents' big station wagon a few hours before the evening they were going home from their weekend visit," The Sperminator recalled. "Some revenge-seeking soul loosened most of the major bolts and connectors on that bike. So, when his folks got home after a long Sunday night drive, all that remained of the mark's expensive mountain bike was the strapped-down frame." The rest had quietly dropped off and rolled away during the nighttime trip.

That's proof to me that if you're an asshole, it doesn't matter which way you peddle; it's going to be uphill and against the wind.

BOOBY TRAPS

At the welcome risk of being branded as an insensitive fool, I must inform you that this chapter is not about brassieres. Uncle Gerry made me include that awful pun.

I admit I haven't thought much about carbon dioxide fire extinguishers until I made the welcome acquaintance of The Kraut, who explained this device's wonderful Haydukery uses, limited only by your imagination about missions and available ammunition.

To turn the carbon dioxide extinguisher (a dry-chemical one will not work as well) into this revenge projector, remove the spreader and replace it with a pipe. Either use a plumbing connector to screw it on, or hold the pipe in place with duct tape. You're now ready to deliver your ammunition to your target/mark. Kraut says you can propel flashlight batteries, ball bearings, ping-pong balls filled with paint, eggs, poop bombs, an M-80/matchhead mixture, almost anything your demented mind desires.

Kraut says this device is no toy, as exit velocity can

be very harmful to soft tissue that gets in the way. He says you had best just read about it here and never, ever do this at home. Or anywhere.

Kraut adds, "I gotta tell you, though, I once heard of a guy in Boston who doused some snooty rich bitch's cats with ink using one of these."

I recall the Big Boppster using one to propel hard goose eggs onto a neighbor's house in Hatboro many years ago.

Equally amusing, Moose told me that he used to replace the contents of those silly gag peanut-brittle cans where spring snakes used to jump out . . . you know, the party-surprise stuff you used to order from Johnson Smith? Moose took out the harmless contents and reloaded with raw eggs, used condoms, beef blood, football player snot, and some truly gross stuff.

As always, Heffer is thinking of the little guy on a limited budget. Ray's come up with a bargain basement activator for only $7.95.

Get a cheapo pocket watch. Pry off the plastic crystal so you can remove the minute and second hands. Replace the crystal. Use a #50 or #60 drill bit to drill a tiny hole in the crystal about where hour 11 is. Place a small screw in that hole, but not touching the watch face.

Attach a small-diameter wire to the screw. Attach another small wire to the watch case body. When the hour hand contacts the screw, you close the circuit and activate whatever device you've attached to the other end of the two wires.

As Heffer says, "You can detonate a little bitsy firecracker or a very big one with this device .   . and very safely, I might add, at least to you."

The New World Order Police keep a tight watch on all sorts of nonsense and humor, such as the type I am mentioning here. Yahweh Clapsattle says to avoid their traps when making your own traps by making your own.

Yahweh was telling me just what Leslie did when she explained nitrogen tri-iodide (N_{13}) to me. It's a hefty explosive that is easily made by mixing equal-volume parts of common household iodine and ammonia and stirring thoroughly. Leslie says that it's totally safe as long as you KEEP IT WET.

"Dry, this stuff is boom-time. A gram of dry mixture can be, uh, temperamental under just its own weight," says Leslie.

Leslie applied liquid N_{13} to toilet seats, car doors, car tires—any area where there could be contact detonation.

Perhaps it's time for some medical attention? Doc Byte's back with his simple formula for a Macelike product that works. Doc says to mix equal parts medical alcohol and iodine and about half as much salt. He says you might want to use a blender to ensure proper mix, as it must be liquid to spray.

Then, you load it into the delivery system of your choice—e.g., Kraut's firing unit, perhaps—and have at it.

Ever consider turning your mark into a tear-jerker, just like TV soaps? Both Steve Hoggard and Kilgore Trout have done just that. Their idea is to buy one of those highly effective handheld CS or tear-gas sprayers so easily purchased these days.

"When your mark has really hurt you and deserves to cry," say Steve and Kilgore, "spray his/her apartment doorknob, car door handles, telephones, toilet seat, whatever.

"It stays active for several hours, and when it comes in contact with skin, the mark will get a burning sensation for half an hour or so. Nothing serious, just irritating."

Finally, on a fun and cutesy note we turn, very uncharacteristically, to Steve Wilson. One of Steve's best friends is also a hard-core snoop who just has to open books, boxes, drawers, letters, anything . . . and look.

Steve cured this by loading an empty videotape box with a small smoke bomb triggered by a simple pressure-relief switch. "I set this up by putting a label on the box that said in big letters: PERSONAL—DO NOT OPEN! So, my pal opened it."

POOOFF . . . mammoth smoke in the room, and mammoth embarrassment for him.

End of problem. And chapter.

BULLIES

Through the years I've learned that most readers prefer to deal with bullies intellectually, i.e., fighting an unarmed enemy. The Eighth Wonder of the World offers an interesting physical alternative, an approach usually out of my genre. Let's make an exception, though, for as Sosi Khui has noted, violence is a giant bulldozer operated by mad people intent on building a road to extinction. Let's help pave that road for the bullies.

Eighth says that those handy little foldaway scissors sold in the notions department of your local mall shop make wonderful brass knuckles. They're sharp, hard, produce ghastly wounds, and they're totally legal to carry.

David from Colorado has a story quite common to many younger readers . . . high school jock bullies. When he tired of their mindless bullying, he snuck a small camera into the locker room and got grand shots of the naked boys doing grab-ass.

"I plastered prints all over school, in hallways, girls' lockers, even in some teachers' desks and on bulletin boards. I put sexual request captions on the pictures, too," David said.

He reports that many of the more postured jocks were given suspensions from school, and there were talks of civil suits by parents of harassed girls. As David said to his trusty camera, "Lens be friends."

Many of the bullies in Madhatter's school were of the Jock Power/Me First persuasion, too, and would pound a pot smoker into the artificial turf, yet thought nothing of doing steroids because, "Uh, Coach said it be wuz good fer me."

Madhatter used to rub a little illegal substance on the lockers of these musclemorons, then have an accomplice from the community notify the police, who brought dope-sniffing dogs into the school.

Even though there were no arrests, the mental damage was done as mistrust was sown between the muscled marks, their parents, police, school officials, and, of course, good old Coach. Madhatter also saw that rumors were begun that good old Coach was the one who dropped the quarter on the boys because they had refused his homosexual advances.

The Reaper detests women beaters and other abusers. Once, he, another guy, and a female friend got one such jerk drunk, then fed him a little sleeping potion until he was very passed out.

"We got him undressed and into female drag . . . clothes, makeup, wig, the whole bit. Then, we shot a lot of nude photos, showing his face. We also showed him blowing one of the guys . . . with only his face showing, of course," Reaper recalled.

They redressed the mark as they found him and took him home. He remembered nothing in the morning. A few days later the photos began showing up at his work site, favorite bar, and parents' home.

According to Reaper, the guy was so broken up and

flabbergasted that he had no idea or recollection of how all of that had happened to him. He swore that the photos were phony. Nobody believed him. People avoided him. His life was never the same, Reaper reports.

CB RADIO

I was afraid that CB was as dead as Seattle Mariner pennant hopes. Some active friends persuade me otherwise. Masterful Merle of satellite TV fame told me about several famous CB renegades, including Fat Ricky.

Fat Ricky didn't like the usual signal radiation antenna that sends the CB radio signal in all directions, so he designed a directional style yagi antenna. That way he could create mayhem on the airwaves, simply changing the directional polarity of his antenna when things got hot.

"To say that he used his CB hookup to give the finger to authority is being very, very mild," said Merle.

Speaking of old masters, Ray Heffer is back with an idea to circumvent laws in many states that prohibit citizens from monitoring police band radios, particularly with a motor vehicle scanner.

Most scanners also have a specific crystal for NOAA weather forecasts. Simply replace that crystal with the local police frequency crystal. Heffer thinks that a fairly knowledgeable friend, perhaps a graduate Radio Shacker, could do his for you quite easily.

Heffer also points out that you can buy those cheap two-, three-, or five-channel CB walkie-talkie units and replace the CB assigned crystals with ones for other frequencies. Do some solid, up-to-date frequency research in your area before trying this one at home, kids.

The benefits are obvious, e.g., less jamming, less crowding, and less monitoring, thus more security for you and your friends. Think about it. By the way, these CBs that use crystals are generally the older models. Newer ones use a frequency synthesizer that restricts you to only the official CB channels.

Ever wish you could talk directly to another vehicle's driver, even if he doesn't have his ears on, good buddy? Bigfoot was following some driver's ed dropout with that thought in mind when he recalled his days as a CB buff. He remembered that it is still legal to operate an FM or AM transmitter with a maximum range of about 100 feet. They used to be called "dorm stations" in the old college days, I believe.

Bigfoot suggests, "You could pack a mobile unit in your car. Then, when some idiot frightens or threatens you with unacceptable driving, you use your mobile transmitter to overpower whatever station he has on the radio and monologue his poor driving.

"If you do this properly and amusingly, the other driver will have no idea idea where 'God' is speaking from, plus you will amuse other drivers who witness the stupid driving," Bigfoot adds.

You could take your verbal cues from car type, bumper stickers, or other decals. Great idea, Bigfoot. Now, let's hear from you Howard Sterns of the freeways.

Experiment, experiment, experiment. But, be careful, as the FCC does not like you to transmit illegally. We should all obey our government.

CHARITY

As we head toward the turn of the new century, charity has become the soured milk of human kindness. It's been a mean-spirited last decade so far, and I see little change.

Steve Wilson told me of a mean mark who used to go out of his way to hassle anyone on relief, welfare, or food stamps. This mark, himself a businessman who took advantage of every form of capitalistic welfare known to the IRS, et al, was especially cruel to welfare children.

Steve says, "In most states it's very illegal to exchange cash for food stamps. So someone set up this mean mark by posting ad fliers offering him as a buyer of food stamps, offering 70 cents on the dollar. Naturally, we made the proper federal gestapo aware of his 'offer' by sending them a copy of his ad."

Steve said they also larded the guy's apartment, through a sympathetic friend, with about $40 worth of food stamps. Steve added, "Then we just sat back and waited for the organic fertilizer to impact the rotary air-moving device."

Mr. MP is another charitable soul. While a member of our beloved military, he often volunteered the services of his marks and markessess to various local charities. He always tried to match his marks with their least favorite charity, e.g. M/Sgt. Homophile for the Friends of Gays Committee.

He also used to donate his marks' properties to charity, sometimes accompanied by official-looking lien papers that caused all sorts of confusion and concern, mostly for the mark.

CHEMICAL

There's a wonderful section in Kurt Vonnegut's hilarious book *Breakfast of Champions* in which a character describes his wife's suicide by swallowing Drano as "Celia became a small volcano, since she was composed of the same sorts of substances which commonly clogged drains."

Drano is, you see, a mixture of sodium hydroxide and aluminum flakes, which, combined with water, will cause a sort of volcanic action to clear drains. Like Celia, perhaps.

All of this literary license was to introduce the chemical section of this book. By the way, all of these chemical funnies and stories have been reviewed for technical veracity by Jim Barclay, who is our Good Hayduking Seal of Approval Chancellor of Chemistry.

In high school art classes, The Queen of Spades was introduced to potassium sulfate, aka liver of sulfur, which was used to tarnish copper. A side effect is a smell that makes skunk and rotten eggs seem charming. Indeed, when combined with warm water, this substance could be applied to various car parts and left to bake in the noonday sun. The Queen says to use your imagination for other uses. Jim Barclay says to use lots of care, because this stuff is as volatile as it gets.

And our old friend, Bob the Liberator, checks in with the thought that drawing a cadmium stick across a piece of aluminum will shortly cause the metal to disintegrate. Bob offers no suggestions, just his vast technical knowledge. Jim also cautions you on this one, adding that this stuff is very toxic.

Sodom worked for a puckered asshole who presented good ideas from employees as his own but blamed his own bad ones on them. One day when the major domo was coming to visit, Sodom got some "detection powder," which is magnesium permanganate, from a police friend. This is the surveillance powder that turns bright purple soon after contact with human skin. And I'm sure you remember my suggestions for its use in earlier tomes.

I bet you can guess Sodom's next move. He says he dusted it very lightly around his boss' office. He adds that you must be very careful not to get any powder on you or your clothing, for obvious reasons.

Have a truly nasty mark whom you wish to give a lasting, personal message? Mr. 3168-44914 has a caustic answer in carbolic acid, aka 88-percent phenol. He's used it to paint obscene or satanic words, signs, or other graffiti on the bodies of passed-out marks. CAUTION: THIS STUFF IS DANGEROUS AND CAN CAUSE BURNS.

Hence, Mr. Lizard suggests that you use simple Karo Syrup, the white variety. It will also corrode and gum things up more cheaply and safely.

Boris got a bad deal on a home appliance, and the dealer totally ignored his complaints. Boris took a plastic injection syringe like a doctor uses and filled it with hydrochloric acid from his paint store. He then had a nasty accomplice enter the mark's store (while Boris was on a business trip with witnesses) and inject the acid into hard-to-locate places on various display appliances.

Major nasty, Boris, major nasty. This rust producer can be used on other hard-to-see surfaces as well.

Remember silver nitrate's contribution to race relations in John Howard Griffin's book *Black Like Me* back in the 1950s? Captain Kirk says to use it sparingly to spotmark your mark. When silver nitrate powder is mixed with water and the solution applied to skin, it is colorless and harmless, although a small amount is absorbed into the skin of your mark.

Exposure to UV light (sun) will turn affected portions of the skin shades of black. Captain Kirk has used this stunt with nasty bikers, offal bosses, and once to make a nasty police dispatcher's ears (from painted earphones) black.

Applications and applicators are limited only by your imagination. And so is the safe and fun use of any of our chemical friends, boy and girls.

COMPUTER

The truly awesome thing about a computer is that it can create the same number of errors in a millisecond as it used to take 100 humans 12 years to do. Some of our friends want to add to that unbenign incapacity.

For example, Tabasco notes that many PCs have a file labeled AUTOEXEC.BAT. This is a batch file that is run automatically when the system is booted. Tabasco says that less than five minutes with your mark's PC will work wonders for that file.

Determine what the system drive is; probably C. At the very end of the AUTOEXEC.BAT file, add the command FORMAT C:. When you do that, the system will continue to operate until the next time it's booted. At such time, the system will execute the AUTOEXEC.BAT command, then when it comes to your added FORMAT C: command, it will merrily write all over itself.

Tabasco's other fun stunt is to expose the circuit boards of your mark's PC, then spray same with liberal doses of antispray liquid of the type used to control static electricity. Let same dry and reassemble the unit. This will create a vast, random network of high-resistance short circuits all through the unit. This same stunt works on most other electronic gear, too, and the real beauty is that there is nothing to repair.

Let's have no smirking when we say that this will cause the system to go down on the mark.

Further folly can be visited upon your mark by following Captain Skellen's command to reset the DIP switches on his or her printer. These are minuscule, tough to locate and manipulate. All the better for you; all the worse for the mark. The printer will create all sorts of graphic garbage when you reset its DIP switches. As a refinement, you might superglue them into the new settings.

Is your mark computer suspicious and less than literate about it? If so, Crazy Ivan would like you to add him or her to the growing horde of BBS folks, you know, electronic bulletin boards. Simply post the mark's name and number on a dozen or so of these networks. Crazy Ivan guarantees a dozen or so calls each night. He test-fired this on one of his landlords who refused to return a safety deposit. It works well.

Have you noticed the growing number of Big Brother balls-ups of our public records systems being credited to "computer error"? Mr. 3168-44914 knows why. And what he knows will amuse you.

A social/political poet, 3168 says that a growing hardcore of antiestablishment fifth columnists are going into government and private sector work as computer feeders, i.e., they input data into the massive computer systems of state motor vehicle bureaus, the IRS, state tax agencies, the personal credit rackets, financial institutions, the military, Social Security, etc. While that's their cover job, their primary mission is to decay the system from within by inputting fucked-up data.

Think about that. A small army of dedicated anti-establishment guerrillas, disguised as computer nerds, is feeding false, misleading, and error-ridden data into these massive systems. And old 3168 is not making that up; it's happening now.

Although I consider him a guru of the universe, 3168 also offers such Earthlike attack methods against a mark's PC as soaking his printer paper in 10-percent sulfuric acid. It's invisible, but it will soon crumble a paper supply. A devotee of China Gordon, 3168 also informs us that lye pellets will quickly destroy aluminum, varnish, and wood, and will create all sorts of system shorts. Would that we could introduce some into the mark's shorts, eh, 3168?

CREDIT CARDS

Speaking of debt, the financial consulting firm of Amy Feinman and Julie Jenkinson told me about the new credit card, American Distress. The card carries the incredibly low annual interest rate of 1 percent, with an annual fee of $8,000.

When a deadbeat left him holding the loser end of a bad business, Ray from Florida used his knowledge of desktop publishing to create professional-quality letterhead and envelopes for a bogus company, then his knowledge of his computer system to access some credit company records for his mark, who had applied for credit with the bogus company.

After getting his mark's confidential credit information, Ray was able to create all sorts of financial mischief for the mark. Stay tuned.

Frank James, and, yes, the original is one of his ancestors, took this idea forward by using a credit rating company as his primary mark and a card "applicant" as his secondary mark. Both deserved his attention because of their theft of his services in a business deal.

"I applied to the hated card company in the name of Mark II, listing his former employer who'd fired him for dishonesty as a current employer. I faked a bunch of information and mixed it in with real data. I had a friend who's a great forger sign Mark II's name," says Frank.

The result was a full-blown credit investigation and some nasty moments involving the credit company, the former employer, a federal agency, plus both civil and criminal attorney types . . . all focused on both marks.

There are several major credit companies, of which TRW is the probably the largest. There is a master computer list of delinquents and other chronic bad credit risks. Most denials of credit are based on derogatory data from this list.

Users of this service report their deadbeats via an 800 number and identifying company codes. Obviously, subscribing businesses have access to this master list of deadbeats.

Get the useful picture here? Mike from Los Angeles says you can use your imagination to create all sorts of credit havoc for your marks. This one is complicated and not for everyone. But, if you've gone beyond printing with crayons, you can create some fun from Mike's lead.

DRUGS

Several narcs I know called George Bush's highly hypocritical war on drugs "The Bush League" for obvious reasons. One of them, now retired, said his employer, DEA, stood for Don't Expect Anything.

I always expect something good from Warhawk, who told me a neat druggie story a few years back. Seems a guy owed him some bucks and wasn't paying. Warhawk got the delinquent on the phone, and they began to chat over old drug stories, with Warhawk prompting the kid to relate some smuggling adventures.

"The putz didn't know I was recording all of this, of course. Then I simply edited out my parts of the conversation," Warhawk said. "I sent the dude a copy of the tape with some vague mentions about copies going to parents, police, etc."

I suspect that sort of thing would really knock your old dick into the dirt. But Warhawk says this kid not only paid his debts but gave Warhawk some pleasant presents as well.

Dr. Deviant says that you can obtain a cactus that

contains mescaline rather easily. The cactus you want is known as *trichocerers pachawoi*. It is available in both cuttings and seed form from several flower supply shops in Arizona and New Mexico (see SOURCES).

After watching those Ad Council TV ads a few years ago, I began to wonder if you could get stoned by frying an egg? Bond 009 fried some crack dealers, though. It's a fun story.

"I wanted them out of our neighborhood, so I bought some chalk and powdered it so it looked like cocaine," Bond 009 relates. "I then packaged it in small electronics-parts Ziplocs. I would then scatter these bags 'carelessly' around the neighborhood playground and school and at the senior citizen center."

He also left a couple in the restroom of the unofficial police station, i.e., Mr. Doughnut, adding, "I opened the bag and spilled some of the powder out near the sink, too."

Two neat things happened. Crackheads found some of the chalk powder, and the police went ballistic because of neighborhood complaints. Bond 0009 had also alerted a local tabloid television station to this Crack Neighborhood story.

The crack house was out of business within the month.

Tit or Tot used to work drug detection canines for the military. He told me a fun trick. Rub snuff or red pepper in your mark's home, vehicle, or clothing. The substance irritates a dog's nose and will cause the animal to react as if there are drugs present. The rest of the mark's hassle seems delightful to contemplate.

Maj. Gen. Gens once got back at a mark by liberating a vial of Rush, a nice liquid buzz, into the offender's small office. Gen says the air was "brain volatile in that little bin." The Rush was circulated a few moments before the mark came to work. Needless to add, it was a short workday.

Ah yes, *drug du jour*, as The Punisher would say.

DRUNKS

Some of my friends and critics are convinced that I have had a ganglion or several separated by an old acquaintance named Jack Daniels. That's one reason I laughed when Ray Heffer told me about getting back at a jerk who served him cheap, spoiled wine at a party.

"I got some Cold Duck—champagne will work, too—and put it in my freezer to get it really cold. Then I set it out and warmed it to room temperature. I did this cycle about half a dozen times, then gave it to the mark. He placed it in his cabinet, where it exploded about a week later. It made quite a mess."

Of course, after hearing of this, our mutual friend Emory Beezak, manager of the local Ghandimart, pointed out that The Prophet is against the use of alcoholic drink. I responded by asking, "But would God allow us to produce this fine quality elixir if She didn't mean for us to use it?"

Emory and I drank to that as we recalled a sad tale from The Chicken Man, who told of a hog of a neighbor who used to drive drunkenly and recklessly into the child-laden residential neighborhood where Chicken Man lived.

"This asshole was a poor driver sober, which was 10 percent of the time, so we placed little orange road sign reflectors on the front of these ornate cement block barriers he had on either side of his wide driveway," Chicken Man related.

"I guess he needed these flags to guide him. So, one night when we knew he'd be cruising in on blotto-pilot, four of us moved each of the pillars in by 3 feet. You got it. He smashed his car into those 300-pound babies at about 20 MPH, bent the shit out of the grill and frame, and wrecked the radiator."

Chicken Man added that because Mr. Asshole never wore a seatbelt, his drunken face got smooshed on the steering wheel, too.

Izzy Stillborne offers another cure for DUI marks. He waits until the jerk has gotten home and parked the car for the night.

"Then, I take an old shirt, lots of fake blood, and a plastic bag of chicken guts to adorn his car. I stick the bloodied shit to the grill after denting it a bit. Then I splash the blood and guts all over the grill and the hood of the car, splashing some on the windshield," Izzy says.

"I have a female friend posing as a police dispatcher call to inform him that his car was reported as being involved in a hit-and-run accident with witnesses. She describes the car, license number, etc."

The call is an attention-getter; the car will be a real eye-opener. The phony dispatcher has told the mark to locate his attorney and surrender at the ____ Street Station immediately.

Happy trials to you, partner.

EXPLOSIVES

When one of Uncle Sam's ordnance experts was teaching me burn-and-blow tradecraft eons ago, he used to hum this catchy little tune called, "When My Full Moon Turns to Gore Again." I wonder, was he referring to our early '90s vice president, who was himself once a soldier?

While the German Duck of Basking Ridge agrees that paintball ordnance is wonderful, he adds that much more can be done with the disposable 12-gram CO_2 cartridges. Duckie says to use a nail to enlarge the hole in the top so you can fill it carefully with black powder. Tamp it carefully, insert a fuse carefully, seal carefully with wax, and you have an explosive device about twice as powerful as an M-80. Be careful, though; lethality kills, as old Nitro Droofik used to point out.

For all you experimenters and welders, Excalibur says to take a large balloon, fill it with a mixture of 50 percent acetylene and 75 percent oxygen, and seal the balloon. Tape a long piece of fuse to the balloon. Attach the balloon to whatever you wish to target, light the fuse, and run like hell. He says the BOOM is quite entertaining.

Lucas from Wisconsin says you can accomplish the same thing by filling the balloon with propane, which is easier for most of us to obtain. Ignite the same way as Excalibur suggests.

For the graduate school of BOOM, though, Excalibur says to use a 20-gallon plastic trash bag and about 4 feet of fuse. Light it and run even faster and farther. He says the results of this one are most mind-boggling and that you should plan to see a lot of fire folks and police arrive shortly after detonation.

Meanwhile, in Utah, dry-ice bombs became popular in the early 1990s, according to Gonville Bromhead, former taste-tester for the Mormon Church Diocese in Bladderwort, Utah. These potentially dangerous bombs are made by placing dry-ice and water in a plastic 2-liter bottle. As the ice "melts," it increases the pressure inside the bottle until the inevitable explosion.

Bromhead reports that several of these dry-ice bombs were used to destroy mailboxes, scatter trash inside Dumpsters, destroy furniture and displays inside offices, and create havoc in institutions, schools, and shopping malls. He told me that these bombs are very powerful and can be quite dangerous.

Because, as The Punisher notes, it's often tough to purchase black powder without ID, he suggests that you purchase model-rocket engines with their fuel cells included in the package. Unwrap 'em, remove the clay, and you've got some good, quality, inexpensive explosive. The Punisher says you can use model-rocket igniters, too. He has used these items to create mammoth flashes and smoke bombs in his mark's charcoal grill, fireplace, wood stove, etc.

The Punisher adds that if you need a nicely timed ignition and are low budget, get a 9-volt battery-powered travel alarm and a solar igniter like kids use with model rockets. Open up the clock, disconnect the actual alarm, and set those wires to the solar igniter. That's it.

Sometimes, though, a bomb doesn't even have to be an explosive. For instance, when he was army-bound, Tit or Tot worked for one of those whiney feminists who demanded equality except when it didn't suit her. Know the type?

Tit or Tot tired of putting up with her and when he had good leave time/location alibi worked out, he secretly got into her office and used duct tape to secure a training grenade (empty and unarmed) under her desk. He attached a trip wire to her chair. He added a typed note to the grenade spoon reading, "Women ARE equal to men, but whiney hypocritical bitches die faster."

There was an investigation, i.e., the U.S. Army Criminal Investigation Division never saw a practical joke it could solve. OK, CID folks . . . your turn?

FEMINISTS

Some years ago I had the stomach-souring displeasure to listen to some female preacher who may still write for *USA TODAY*, the fast-food version of American journalism, tell us that real men are feminists. As a pioneer supporter of the Equal Rights Amendment and all that it entails, and as a firm believer in equal reward for equal work, risks, etc., I thought she was full of fresh, unprocessed fertilizer. I also once worked with a sensitive little weenie who called himself a male, plus a mighty assistant professor, no less, who felt a biological urge to sit down to relieve its bladder. Before he was born, his father had wanted a little girl while his mother wanted a boy. I guess they're both happy.

That's all offered as a prelude to an interesting suggestion from Barney Vincelette as to how men can protect themselves from those dangerous fringe feminists whose sole aim is to violently emasculate men, i.e., ones who don't have to sit down to pee.

Relax. From the get-go, Barney's idea is all in fun, like this book, for entertainment purposes only. It goes like this.

Barney says you have to watch out for those violent feminists whose favorite attack mode is walk up to some poor schulck who's minding his own business, paying no attention to her for any reason, and, when in range, deliver a life-snatching kick to his testicles, driving them so far into his body that he'll have four eyeballs, two of them black and blue, for seven months.

Here's how ovary-busting Barney will turn that ball-shattering kick into real revenge. He suggests having a heavy steel cup made with a piece of 1/4-inch plumbing pipe brazed to the outside of the cup. A 12-gauge shotgun shell with attached striker and outer-spring is mounted inside the pipe. When the attacker directs her kick, the man shifts the target area so the attacker's shoe hits the spring-loaded shell, driving it into the pipe and against the striker.

BLLAAAOOOOOMMM!!!!!!!!!

The feminist attacker's foot resembles a flesh, bone, and blood salad shooter.

As I said, it is an R-rated cartoon fantasy. As Winston Churchill once had to tell Iron Margaret Thatcher, "Yo, Maggie, if you can't take a fuck, joke ya'."

But to more serious matters. From his myriad trips around the world, The Squire reports the results from his scholarly research into Feminology. The Squire found that seven of every ten men who participated in his survey liked the way they looked naked, while only two of ten women said they liked the way they looked naked. He interviewed 2,300 people in public bath houses internationally. He also reports that women make three times as many telephone calls as men. But then, we already knew that.

In the eighteenth century, there was a midwestern Indian tribe that punished a squaw who committed adultery by letting every male or female who wished have sexual relations with the woman in public, one after the other. If she survived that, then, fine, the sentence was served. The guilty male? He had already been executed immediately after the verdict was decided by the elders.

Savages?

As a final suggestion, The Chicken Man says that the next time some femcommando gets on your nerves and tells you that a woman can do anything a man can do, and do it better, ask her to piss in a long-neck bottle without using a funnel.

HOME

Max and Terry Sink swear that they were there when this happened, and as they are good old black powder and fiddlin' boys, who am I to question whether or not they were there.

They said this truly gorgeous babe walked into the neighborhood bar the other night when it was filled with regulars, all guys.

"Boys, I will do it all, for free, tonight for one of you," she purred in a husky voice. "I get $1,000 a night; I'm that good. Tonight, I'll do anything one of you wants, for free, all night long, just for you."

Then, this stunning doll, a Cindy Crawford look-alike in a clinging jersey sundress cut low in front and high in hem, strolled past the stunned, nervous, and obviously awed men. Terry and Max said she looked like liquid Jello walking.

"There wasn't a flaccid member in the place," Max coughed with humorous relief at the mammary, err, memory.

She stopped in front of one guy, who practically

swallowed his adam's apple, paused, then said, "You! I choose you. I'll do whatever you want, better than you've ever had it before, all night long. What did you want me to do?"

The guy stared right into her eyes, then said in a near whisper, "Uhhh . . . paint my house?"

OK, so your home is more than just a place to eat, sleep, and walk around in your underwear. It can also be the scene of some fun Haydukery. Matt the Lizard points out that the kitchen is one of the most vulnerable locales in the home, e.g., adding light motor oil to olive oil, laundry soap in the salt, urine in the salad oil, etc. Yup, the kitchen is indeed a buffet of creativity serving up myriad options of nastiness.

Captain Chaos likes to put his mark seriously in the dark by replacing regular screw-in fuses with Buss Fustats. These little gems use an adapter that fits a standard screw-in socket and are practically impossible to remove once you've made the conversion. Of course, a dab of Loktite will make them totally impossible to remove.

Both Naomi and Rev. Mitchell suggested that you might want to break into your own home, trash it a bit, even breaking a few things you don't really care about. Of course, you want to leave around a lot of evidence that your mark was there and did the dirty deed. Call the police.

Naomi suggested further that you make prior arrangements to meet your mark at your place for some bogus reason, then call the police about 10 minutes before the mark is to arrive.

You can always invite some of your mark's friends in the KKK or from Satan to help, too.

Nathan Begerlind says if your mark owns a large piece of wooded land, you can clear a small area in the deeper woods, add a fire pit, and a rough-hewn shack.

Party there with some friends so the locale looks well used, Nathan adds.

Place litter, e.g., stained underwear (including that of children), alcohol, drug paraphernalia, plus literature and icons from the Klan, a satanist cult, voodoo, mutilated animal carcasses, porno pictures, photo composites of local biggies, drafts of letters threatening local officials, etc.

Next, a call to local TV news operations is in order. Have a friend make the call and tell the reporters that "you" accidentally stumbled over this place while hunting. Then call the local cops. All of this is done from a pay phone. Tell them that "your" name is Sarah Bradee or something odd like that.

Watch the 11 o'clock news for "your" story. Enjoy your mark's cheesy explanations.

A nonfriend made a mess of The Cootie's kitchen. He returned her favor by heating a hardboiled egg in her microwave. Actually, he let her do it. Overdone just a tad. It exploded with enough force to blow the door open. It also left a real mess inside the microwave.

INSULTS

Like graffiti and other nasties, these can be tossed against your mark's ego in person, blamed on others, or done anonymously. As Omar Shabazz noted in the introduction to his Ph.D. dissertation, "Doing the Dozens in South Philadelphia: Life Is Its Own Past Self," good insults will cement the relationship between enemies, even if one doesn't know it.

I offer these insults for your consideration as a mix-and-match set, or as brain fodder for your own creative expression, be it verbal, written, published, graffito, bumper-stickered, or whatever medium you choose. The medium will make you happy. Feel free to fill in your own blanks.

- If a pompous asshole of either gender asks you, "Do you know who I am?" Your answer is polite, "No, but I shall make inquiries and inform you directly."
- A _____ and a _____ both jump out of an airplane at the same time. Who splats all over the countryside first? (Who cares?)
- Two _____ went to the drive-in? They didn't like the film so they slashed their seats.

- What do you say to a ____ in a three-piece suit? (Will the defendant please rise.)
- If Tarzan and Jane were _____, what would Cheetah be? (The smartest of the three.)
- What do you find in a _____'s nose? (Fingerprints.)
- How can you identify a ____ firing squad? (They're the ones standing in a circle.)
- The well of _____'s intellect is a shallow puddle.
- _____ grew up in a genetic cul de sac.
- I've just learned of _____'s illness and I hope it's nothing trivial.
- _____ isn't worthy to suck boogers from a _____'s nose.
- Why do _____ wear hats? (So they know which end to wipe.)

When a friend of Susan and Millie retired and began to hang around the house all day getting in the way, his wife bought him a sweatshirt with a French word emblazoned across the front. She told him it was French for RETIRED.

When he showed up back at the office to show off his sweatshirt, which he now wore everywhere, one of his former co-workers who spoke fluent French told him that the word on the front of his shirt did not mean "retired." The word was French for HORSE'S ASS! True story; use it or abuse it.

By the way, there is an insult club. It's called The International Maledicta Society, 331 S. Greenfield Avenue, Waukesha, WI 53186. They are interested in clever forms of blasphemy, insults, slurs, and other like-minded fans.

And, my final contribution to your insult armament for this issue: I wouldn't piss up _____'s ass if his guts were on fire.

INSURANCE

Next time an insurance salesthief promises to be your friend, cover your backside and run. Or do as Marty the Alchemist did. Using someone else's desktop publishing, he created a national insurance company boycotting organization, complete with a board of WASPish directors, letterhead, and several addresses and telephone numbers in key cities, including international centers of commerce.

"The phones rang in to friends who were in on my scam. I sent the bogus letterhead to offending companies, the content of the letter being that 'we' had received numerous complaints from their customers.

"I also mentioned that we were asking various regulatory agencies to get involved and were querying the Justice Department about possible RICO violations," Marty explained.

From a friend inside one of the companies, Marty learned that the result of this bogus campaign was rampant paranoia, followed by a real cloak 'n dagger operation to find "the real story."

As Marty explained, "Those uptight, puckered ass-holes never tumbled that this was just a scam to waste their time and increase their personal levels of stress."

A grand, premium stunt, Marty. Kudos to you, sir!

The Brown Hornet did much the same thing to pay back several faulty insurance companies in California. His biggest contribution was mass distribution of a very realistic-looking official state government document that "legalized" nonpayment of premiums and authorized personal liability lawsuits against sales agents, claim settlers, and company officials. It was all a hoax, but it created panic within the insurance industry and their paid pals, the pukepols, in Sacramento.

By the way, if you're interested in whacking back at the insurance industry, please read Harold F. Willard's book *Insurance Ripoffs and Dirty Tricks* (Thumbsdown Books, P.O. Box 961, Kirkland, WA 98083-0961).

JAIL

The good Rev. Nastyman definitely knows from up close that more legal cases are decided between urinals than jurors.

With Fortress America dumping more and more of her citizens into our biggest national growth industry, prisons, each month, mail privacy has become a major concern with more and more family and loved ones still on the outside. According to the government's own stats, America has the highest per capita percentage of its population in prison than any other country in the world.

Our beloved Constitution is probably the finest thought-out and written document in human history. And it works well . . . on paper. But so does Monopoly.

A few brave folks have volunteered suggestions for keeping personal mail just that. The Red Wild Head says to mail sealed personal correspondence in an official-looking legal envelope with a printed return address that reflects some official in the criminal justice system. Mark the outer and inner envelope as OFFICIAL/CONFIDENTIAL.

For example, Khi Dot uses the return address of

Judge Gonif Dipperbrine, 69th Circuit Court, Poontang County Courthouse, Sphincter, MI, or, well, you get the real idea, I suppose.

Here's one for the booking room, and it comes from The Phantom. Those of us who've been printed know that fingerprint ink is very black, very gooey, very spreadable, is a chore to remove from one's hands, and is almost impossible to remove from other objects.

The Phantom's list of other suggested markable objects include clothing, toilet seats, doorknobs, telephone receivers, etc. This ink is available through law enforcement supply houses (see SOURCES).

To slam the door on this section, we repeat the immortal words of $$ Bill from Attica, who points a knowing index finger with cocked thumb, aims, and says laconically, "BANG! Ya' know?"

JOCKS

Smile; every seven minutes of every day, one of those sweaty, accessory-attired Ken and Barbie Hardbody aerobic machines pulls a hamstring big time.

While big-time baseball has promoted everything but Boat People Day or Hit a Homer for the Homeless, Mike from LA has an explosive idea that he credits to the Big League bat-corkers. He says it works, too.

Drill out a bat as if to cork it, only fill the cavity with about about 3 ounces of black powder, tamp it really well, and top with some matchheads of the strike-any-where variety. Seal the seam.

If the mark connects solidly with a pitch anywhere near that seam, well, only God and the team laundry folks will know just how scary that trick can be.

It's amazing how much rip-off is now involved in the sports card collection industry. Nimrod says people even print counterfeit cards because the prices for the real things are so high. A dishonest dealer ripped off Nimrod a few times, who got even by "helping" this man.

"I planted some packs of truly worthless, bogus, and

poorly counterfeited cards at his table, all sealed in the premier wrappers. I included them with his prime rate (expensive) inventory. By the end of the show, the F word (fraud) was flying along with his name all over the hall. He had a dozen complaints, two threatened lawsuits, and the police had been called," Nimrod noted.

I used to think my collection of Richard Nixon Lies was vast and valuable, but I've since learned that all of the baseball cards I had as a kid back in the 1940s and 1950s are worth a lot of money. And, yeah, I really do have them all.

Have you a least favorite surfer? Could there be? Matt the Lizard has a helpful hint. He explains that a surfboard is a piece of fiberglass coated with a resin compound to protect the fiberglass' Styrofoam interior from absorbing water.

"Absorption of water causes delamination, which ruins a surfboard," Matt tells us. "A water-filled syringe will pierce the resin compound and introduce water to the Styrofoam. The more water, the more damage as the result. New boards cost from $200 to $400."

Biggus saw a bodybuilder humiliate a mutual friend. Biggus attended a party at the bodybuilder's place, and, while others were distracted, he quickly went to the man's weight machine, set the weight keys to the heaviest setting, then bent the keys so they couldn't be removed.

Muscle types who like to break things irritated you lately? Rev. Nastyman, a martial arts disciple, has some suggestions from his studies. If your mark breaks boards, reinforce them with metal rods or a coat of lacquer. Replace older, weaker bricks that Mr. Macho will crack with fireplace bricks. This stunt can break the mark's hand. If your mark likes to break ice blocks for his macho act, he may cheat and salt the block first. Substitute sugar for his salt.

My friend Bronko Queed and I belong to Athletes Anonymous. Anytime we get the urge to work out, one calls the other, who shows up with a case of cold beer and an evening of funny stories about the old days.

LANDLORDS

M r. Mondo's mark was the elfin-looking hench-
man for a typical college town slumlord, i.e.,
his superintendent. This super for Mondo's building was
a tiny, lazy lush who never did any work and complained to all who'd listen about the sick, crazy tenants
"who outta be taken out and blown up."

"I tired of him and decided to do some mindfucking.
Since he never cleaned, I thought to give him some personal motivation by neatly painting personalized graffiti
around the building," Mr. Mondo explained.

He used phrases like FUCK OFF RUNT; DIE NAZI
RUNT; EAT TINY TURDS, RUNT; GROW BALLS, RUNT
. . . stuff like that. He also had a friend neatly letter
RUNTMOBILE on the super's car.

"For my finale, I got up to the building's roof and
painted in huge red letters THE RUNT SUCKS on the
vertical elevator shaft that faces the city and on the roof
itself, which is lower than all of the surrounding build-
ings," Mr. Mondo said.

The little super scurried around cleaning the graffiti.

The slumlord's business pals laughed at him about this, and Mr. Mondo told me that they had a tenants meeting and got some changes made, i.e., a new super.

Krazy Kaliko had a nasty landlord who constantly berated and belittled tenants, including sexually insulting females who refused his advances. Krazy decided when a semisecondary mark was moving from his apartment, he would become a potato farmer.

"The landlord was a shit, and this tenant who was moving was his asshole buddy, so I decided to plant 'em both," Krazy told me. "I got some of the those small, new potatoes and stuffed them down into the water drains, then put a little water on top so the spuds would absorb this and swell."

The results of this hydroponic gardening were awesome. First, the wet spuds swelled into the pipes, creating a tight seal that caused flooding whenever any water was turned on. Then, as the tubers began to rot in a few days, they started to smell as only a rotted potato can smell. Ugh. The main crop, of course, was a happy plumber flush with megamoney from repiping the apartment.

Others take revenge more lightly. For example, before he moved, Dennis the Menace superglued all the lightbulbs into their sockets because his landlord refused to do maintenance.

The Avid Avenger bombarded a landlady who used to unplug his refrigerator to save electricity without caring that his food might spoil. When he prepared to move, Avid left a little message for her.

"I wired the contacts from a 120v SPDT relay to the prongs of her refrigerator plug, then connected one side of the switch contact to two AA batteries and the other contact to a small firecracker's fuse. I wanted to scare her, not blow up her room," Avid reports.

Finally, Mr. Pinaphicus used his fellow tenants' hatred of the landlord to have some fun. He printed some official looking NOTICE OF ENTRY doorhangers that read as follows:

ON _____, I_____entered your residence for the official purpose of _____.

Mr. Pinaphicus filled in the date, the landlord's name, then wrote various purposes on various hangers and attached them to tenants' doors in random fashion. Some of the purposes included TO STEAL, TO MASTURBATE IN YOUR MILK, TO TAKE A SHIT, TO WEAR YOUR WIFE'S UNDERWEAR, TO FANTASIZE ABOUT MAKING LOVE TO YOUR CHILD, etc
Needless to say

LAND RAPE

Suburban housing developments are always named after the wonderful creations of nature that the developers destroy to create their hideous yuppieville monstrosities. Many of them even truck in artificial replacements, e.g, plastic trees. My old pal Heffer from Kansas City has offered to help nature.

Styrofoam peanuts are a plentiful by-product of our plastic age. Heffer says you can buy them commercially by the hopper full. Locate your unfavorite land rapist's newly opened development and help him decorate with the Styrofoam.

Heffer suggests, "You'll need several pickup trucks filled with garbage bags of the little decorations, plus a dark and windy night. Just open the bags and let nature and the peanuts help you pay back the bastard who messed up the real landscape.

"The next morning the place will look like a hailstorm hit it. But the real fun starts at cleanup . . . it's impossible. You can't rake those little guys, nor can you suck 'em up with a commercial vacuum. Nope. It's one-at-a-time handwork."

One of my least favorite sounds is the snowmobile, a possibly useful machine that is most often turned into a noisy, air-polluting winter toy for knucklewalkers. My friend Doobie Nixon, a resident of Litsko, Minnesota, hates these motorized cretins who invade her wooded homeland, too. She spreads monofilament line trails for them when they trespass in her woods. The line gets sucked into the machine's mechanism and puts a rapid stop to this desecration of her home.

Glass-etching cream is a splendid product to deliver an unmistakable message to a land rapist's office, home, or vehicle's glassy parts. Teeter Combs owed a clearcutter who ruined ole Teeter's water supply, so he used etching-cream bombs, which he created by using standard chicken and goose eggs.

Teeter says, "Cut the end off the egg with a very sharp razor, dump out the contents to use in a cake or something tasty, then dry out the egg. Later, spoon in etching cream, lay tissue paper over the cut end, then gently seal that with melted wax or rubber cement."

Wear gloves, of course.

According to Teeter these little bombs leave a truly ugly splattering scar on any glass or plastic they touch.

And the beat goes on for these enemas of our wonderful planet with their "good jobs/good development" bullshit. Dr. Chow Sow Jee, an environmental ordnance specialist with the Hayduke Institute of Semiology, tells of the use of an "acetylene grenade" that disables large yellow machines.

"If the machine is very large, you may have to use one of those Benzomatic-sized tanks of acetylene, or simply fill a smaller balloon with the product. Then introduce it into the air cleaner assembly of a diesel engine. When the engine is started, the balloon and its product are sucked into the induction system. The fuel ignites prematurely and could break a piston rod," Dr. Chow Sow Jee says.

Exxon . . . changing the face of the world, forever, I fear.

LAUNDRY

Roommates who use your clothes without asking should be taken to the cleaners. Captain Prickman did just that when a former roomie moved to a new address. He bought one of those sample-size laundry soaps sold in laundromats. Next, he went to the drugstore and bought a box of the ugliest dye he could find.

The good Captain says, "Carefully slice open the bottom of the laundry soap box and dump out some of the powder. Add the dye and mix well. Use a thin coat of good glue to reseal the box.

"Then, add a fake mailing label to OCCUPANT and place in the mark's mailbox. At least, that's what I did. Ahh yes, whiter whites and brighter colors, all mixed up."

He also thought of trying this same stunt with a drain opener. But that sounds dangerous and damaging.

In another corner of the laundromat, Biggus Piraphicus mused on the efficacy of mixing superconcentrated skatole, mercaptan, or, perhaps, carbide with fabric softeners. He also figured out a way to clump his mark's detergent, i.e., using a syringe and needle to inject water forcefully into the box and . . .

Greg McGary is an artist who has an appreciation for the tie-dyed-died effect of the 1960s. Indeed, he told of a friend who tried to help some evil marks who'd ripped him off achieve good clothes karma.

"He took some crayon pieces and scattered them inside of the dryer drum, where there're lots of holes. He said that the sheets and clothes of his enemies had that great '60s look . . . all for free."

When Marc Beck moved into an apartment complex, two of his neighbors were those rude sorts who would remove his clothes from his washer or dryer and substitute their own. He said, "It was as if to say 'I'm important, kid, and so's my laundry. Screw you and yours' to me," he said.

The first couple of times, Marc turned the other cheek. It was the third time that made him think of red food coloring and beef bouillon cubes.

"I waited a good few weeks, using other laundry facilities, but noted that other residents complained about the same two slobs. So I watched and waited. Then, when they loaded in their goodies and left, I added my little color makers . . . and I left," Marc said.

LOCKS

A knave once had the nerve to pinch personal items belonging to our very own Captain Picard. Foolish twit, that knave. The Captain simply located the fool's room key whilst the mark was passed out from drink, made several duplicate keys, then spent the next eight or ten weeks recovering the stolen items plus appropriate compensatory interest and punitive damages.

"Not only did I retrieve my stolen goods over this period of time, but I 'borrowed' some of his as well. As he'd taken cash from me in the form of unpaid small loans, I paid myself back from his wallet, plus a few CDs, videos, etc."

Picard continues, "The secret here is to take only a little bit at a time so the mark doesn't suspect. I cleared about a 200-percent profit on his dishonesty. Also, I was very covert about my operations."

One of Captain Prickman's former friends damaged our friend's car and refused to pay for repair. Without more than simmering anger, the Captain had back at his cheap foe. By continuing to be nice to the idiot, Prickman obtained a copy of the guy's car key, his house key, and his office key, plus the key to his girlfriend's (unknown to mark's wifey) apartment.

The Captain got those little metal "return to" tags printed for the myriad copies of each key The tags listed the mark's name, address, and mention of a $20 cash reward for the safe return of "lost" keys. He then disseminated these items around town

"I tried to locate these little treasures in areas that might shelter some of our community's less desirable elements in hopes that I might play Robin Hood," the Captain added.

We've all faced the school bully in one or more of his/her stupid guises. The Professor tired of this and, being smarter than the bully, was able to jimmy open the animal's hall locker. He stuffed some drug- and porn-related contraband inside, then relocked the thing with the same school-issue combination lock.

"That's when my fun started," The Professor said. "I used heavy black paint to cover over the raised white numbers totally. The idiot could not see to open his locker and arrogantly commanded a hall monitor to fetch the custodian to open the lock."

We'll leave The Professor's story now, as I'm sure you're already chuckling over the next scene, the one featuring the principal, the ashen bully, the police, parents, et al.

Want to bollocks up someone's lock quickly and easily without carrying incriminating evidence like glue tubes? A good, literate gentleman who spent 30 years as "a special agent protecting the rights of his fellow citizens" outlined a splendid method.

Roll a tiny piece of aluminum foil into a thin sliver. Push this sliver into the keyhole of the mark's lock with a toothpick. When the mark inserts the key, it pushes the tiny bit of foil the rest of the way in, and it seems as if the key is home. Twist and turn every which way, yet the lock just won't open.

If it's an expensive lock, it will cost $$$ to get it fixed. And unless there is complete disassembly of the lock, the sliver will never be found. Repeat as you will . . . old or new locks, it always works.

MAIL

Mildred Marie told me about her old neighborhood pal who used to get back at mail order companies that ripped him off by allowing the U.S. Postal Service to be his ally. Here is Mildred's version of his story.

"You got ripped off? From the same company, order lots of CDs on a SEND NO MONEY deal using a false name and P.O. box. When you get your CDs, immediately file a change of address using that fake name and some secondary mark's address. Mail it and forget it. Enjoy your CDs."

The company will eventually give up trying to figure out who is who and who got what where. But remember, some grown-ups might consider this to be mail fraud. So don't really do it, just chuckle at Mildred Marie's friend.

Darren Ankenman says he used to purchase 1-cent or 5-cent stamps that looked similar in color and design to the regular first-class letter stamp. He said that 99 percent of the time the letters got through fine, cutting his postal costs amazingly. Perhaps we could pass Darren's ideas along to our elected things whose wasteful political mailings are nothing short of mail prostitution. We should be frank-incensed over political mailings!

Handgun Control is a slimy bunch of pukes. The German Duck of Basking Ridge agrees. After he saw the rather hefty fines for attempting to reuse canceled stamps, he mutilated a bunch of canceled stamps pretty well by trying to erase the cancellation ink. Then he wrote some letters to asshole groups like Handgun Control, the Democratic/Republican National Committees, Corporate NBC, Time/Life, Donald Wildman's dingbats, etc., and used the stamps to try to mail them. The return addresses were all marks with similar leanings as the companies to whom the letters were being sent. He also tried reversing the roles a few times. A friend inside the post office told The Duck that a postal inspector was on the case within the week.

Need to get into a sealed envelope surreptitiously? Captain Picard suggests wetting the sealed flap portion, then nuking the missive in a microwave for 30 seconds at medium high. It will steam open the letter.

With the letter steamed open, Picard does all sorts of tricks involving porn, live insects, returned mail, mail forwarded, etc. Let your imagination be your guide.

Need help finding organizations and associations with which to offend your mark via mail? Follow Louisiana Sunshine's advice—go to your local or college library and consult the *Encyclopedia of Associations*. Every group in the world is listed, along with a brief synopsis, mailing address, and telephone number. Have fun with this valuable information, Haydukers, and thank Louisiana Sunshine for sharing it.

Bill Harrison told me about a friend of his who used

to send his tamer marks odd bits of weird stuff from odd places. It worries most people to get a piece of sandpaper, one old glove, haircut detritus, half an old necktie, a diaper, an oddball or obscure church bulletin, etc., in the mail with a very odd postmark, e.g., East Bumfuck, AZ; Snot, FL; Roberta's Corners, WV; Dork, MN, etc.

Most members of the woebegone human race are irrationally afraid of specific creatures, as both Matt the Lizard and George Orwell have pointed out. Matt says the addition of harmless and nonvenomous snakes and spiders with big hair and/or body mass into the mark's mailbox after the USPS employee has made the daily rounds will cause lots of active fun.

Gentle and kindly Uncle Hugh once did this with a cat that had been terrorizing small animals and birds in the neighborhood. After his daily dip into the medicinal spirits, Uncle Hugh captured this caustic kitty and stuffed it, squalling, into the owner's mailbox. Both owner and kitty required emergency medical treatment following discovery of the animal in its new home after an hour of enclosed residence.

In doing an after-action critique, gorgeous and deceptively soft-spoken niece Sandy suggested that next time Uncle Hugh use a rabid animal.

Want to use the USPS to play detective for you? Doyle is a former investigator and offers the following for you:

- To find where your mark has moved and to get the new address, send a letter to the mark at the old address and use your mail drop name/address as the return. You must also type these exact words in all caps at the bottom of the envelope: ADDRESS CORRECTION REQUESTED. Your letter will be forwarded to the mark, plus the USPS will send you a form with the mark's new address.

- If you want only the form and do not want the mark to get your letter (you get it returned to you), then at the bottom type in all caps ADDRESS CORRECTION REQUESTED. DO NOT FORWARD.
- Need the name and street address of a business holding a P.O. box? Use the FOIA and write to the local postmaster and inquire who holds box as well as what the street address of record is. They will do this only for business boxes, not for individuals' boxes.

MALLS

As my good friend and intern in curmudgeonry P.J. O'Rourke told me, "My hometown, Toledo, is gone . . . replaced by a mall." Yes, if only Sherwood Anderson could see our town now.

That the ubiquitous mall has taken over America is obvious. In fact, one of the new entries in *McManmon's New Scatalogical Dictionary* notes the word *maltigo* and defines it as "a temporary state of confusion upon exiting a mall shop and not knowing from which direction one entered."

Do you enjoy it when some drekbrain angles his valuable car across two parking spaces to keep others from parking too close? Joe Ling drives a shitty old dump of a truck and doesn't care. So he parks at the same angle about 4 inches from the other car's driver side door, blocking entry for the asshole driver.

Or how about the cretin who blocks the entrance to a crowded parking lot lane waiting for the next available space close to the mall? Simply drive up the next lane, then back down in front of the cretin and take the next spot yourself.

One of Biggus Piraphicus' marks played Mall Santa a Christmas ago. Little kiddies would be interviewed by Santa's helpers, who would write brief notes about what each kiddie wanted so Santa could read them if the child froze or went ballistic at the key moment. Show biz, you know.

Biggus said, "I was able to intercept some of the real notes and substitute some of my own. These asked Santa for sex toys, or told him to fondle the child, or that the child's parent wanted Santa to perform a bizarre sex act with that parent or spouse."

Biggus said that six such incidents happened the first two days, and a bewildered, then insanely furious Santa was fired.

Dick Croup had an acquaintance named Brown Bag who was furious with a mall drugstore for cheating him on an insurance claim. During the local "health week," this store had one of those blood-pressure devices that you inserted your thumb into to get a pressure reading, which a store clerk recorded for you.

Brown Bag waited until his mark, the female manager of the store, was seated at the blood-pressure cuff. After a brief bit of mental and guarded physical preparation, Brown Bag was up and ready. He approached his mark and her machine, then carefully inserted his erect penis in the cuff.

Dick says, "The screaming, confusion, and laughter was so great that Brown Bag easily reclothed Mr. Happy and strolled out of the store and the mall."

Queenie had made hang-up and nasty calls to some really nice people, so Dr. Death set straight this case of trouble. She self-printed 500 letter-sized posters, which she hung all over each shopping mall in a two-town area.

The poster invited folks to win prizes worth up to $100 cash, thanks to ____, and here Dr. Death used a secondary mark, a mall shop with whom she'd had hassles. The rest of the poster told folks that all they had to do was call ____, and here she listed Queenie's home telephone number, adding that contest phone lines would be open from 6 P.M. until midnight. Next, each caller was instructed to ask for ____, which was Queenie's first name, and say, "Aren't you glad you use your phone properly?" The final instruction was to keep calling, as the more you call, the better your chances of winning.

Gosh, could you get into trouble for doing that? That's kind of like getting arrested for trying to smuggle library books into the mall. You'd be freed on a technicality because none of the residents there could recognize a book.

MEDIA

One of my all-time favorite heroes is H.L. Mencken. The assholes for the 1990s, aka the politically correct gestapo and thought police, call him a racist and an antisemite. Crawl back under your rocks, you illiterate dumbfucks. Mencken didn't like anyone very much, and he would have shredded you prissy popcorn farts, splitting your sensitive infinitives and cutting off your dangling participles.

In 1952, Mencken wrote the most accurate description I have yet read of the media industry, noting, "The difference between burlesque and newspapers is that the former never pretended to be performing a public service . . ."

I used to respect the media industry when it stood for something other than corporate profit while fucking its employees and the public. Today, I am saddened by its infotainment, its twinkie talking heads, its lack of ethics, its refusal to ask the tough questions, and its pandering to sensationalism.

But, I digress.

No longer will I call that industry "the media." From now on, it will be known as the Infotainment Industry. So, let's start this chapter again.

INFOTAINMENT

There are some truly neat people who do work in the industry. Barry Young is absolutely the funniest talk-show person I've ever known over these past many years. Jeff Charles is a close second. For all his big-league television success, Jay Thomas remains one of nicest. Tina and Jack from Fargo, North Dakota, made me feel really welcome and run a class act. Frosty Stillwell in Milwaukee is a great guy, too, fun and real. Ditto for Paul Baker of WHP in Harrisburg, who proved to me that there is humor in the rusted wasteland of Pennsylvania.

Until I'd met Kevin McManus, I thought everyone who worked for the the *Washington Post* was a pencil-necked Beltway schmuck. Kevin is a damn good journalist, like the old days, and a helluvan honest, decent guy. Wonder how he stands the pompous fucks he works for? I'm not alone in my feelings. Alice Kahn of the *San Francisco Chronicle* is a funny lady and great writer who keeps her word.

Nimrod doesn't like newspaper monopolies, and he gets some big laughs by thinking of imaginary ways to hassle them. Once he asked me, humorously, of course, why tamper with newspaper machines to swipe a damn 50-cent newspaper? Nimrod says to cut the security chain with bolt cutters and cart the entire vending unit away. And keep the change, too.

Mike from LA is also a serious kidder. He once found a way to seriously embarrass a local talking head twinkie who pissed off real people by his show-biz TV style that prostituted real journalism.

Mike says, "I found out his favorite bar and scoped out the action . . . did some recon. On Strike Night I had a friend who was a very good amateur actor go into the bar just after Mr. TV Twinkie, then go into his 120 dB performance as the mark's jilted male lover.

Some sample monologue follows . . . for humor purposes only . . .

"I'm glad you ran out on me, you limp-cocked wastebasket. You don't even make your new honeyboy wear a rubber while he buttfucks you. Did you tell *him* about your AIDS, pencil penis?"

You probably see where this one is heading . . .

The Butler is currently a reporter for a large-market daily newspaper. He says the media are big on other folks' misfortunes and civil liberties and act as everyone's watchdog but their own.

In Kansas City, for example, management routinely runs drug tests and once brought a drug-sniffing dog into their newsroom. The Butler told me that the editor and the publisher began to receive boxes and bags of dogshit on a regular basis from that day on.

I really liked the Butler's idea that uses the gullibility and stupidity of many of the underpaid and undereducated drek now being hired by the media as cheap labor. He says to dress up in a suit and either come into the offices or hold a news conference at a local motel suite. Represent yourself as a government official or whatever. Have bogus credentials.

"Then, give them all sorts of bogus claims, stupid opinions, and outright lies. Misrepresent some politicians, make dollar promises . . . feed them the type of crap that they love to disseminate to the public," The Butler says.

He cautions not to make a burlesque out of it, though. He also points out dozens of examples of media hoaxes each year. Some of the topical areas that most reporters are woefully ignorant in are military affairs, international politics, geography, gun control (as most media types are rabid antigunners, this one is easy), drunken drivers, gangs, street crime, the local drug war, etc.

The Punisher's friend worked for a radio station that wrongfully fired him, then denied it, saying he'd quit to prevent him from getting the unemployment benefits to which he was entitled. This same station ran a lot of these "Call the Listener and Ask 'What's your favorite radio station?' Say Us and Win a Prize" promotions.

Using various pay phones, Punisher called lots of citizens at random times, pretending to be the station. Very simple, very effective, very nasty, very deserved in this case.

Naomi has one that works well in small-market radio. Call in requests for sappy songs with sappy dedications for your mark's spouse from his/her lover (your choice). In a small town, there are few secrets and lots of rumors.

As a student journalist, Roberto Venganza loved to create imaginary campus incidents which involved all of the politically incorrect subjects, then quote both imaginary and real campus people about the situations. He was able to offend almost all of the sensitive sacred cattle on campus, and thus anger to action the very formidable PC police on his campus.

How did he do it? He made it all up. He'll go far in the corporate Infotainment Industry, i.e., someone who can talk a squirrel down out of a walnut tree. And I hope he does . . . we need more Haydukers prodding those suitmen.

Dick Smegma reports that if your local newspaper refuses to run your letter or ad, go to a print-it-yourself shop and publish it as a one-page flyer. Then, simply insert your addition into copies of the paper at local convenience stores and newsstands. If asked what you're doing, tell them it is a forgotten insert you need to add. Maybe they'll help you. It was done to *The Houston Chronicle*.

As I get older, I find myself looking at the obit column in the local newspaper before I even read the headlines. I also find my mind wandering back to the old days and all of the newspaper people who were so supportive of me by doing stories in their papers about my early books.

Here is a roster of those newspaper folks I want to thank for help getting me started a long time ago:

Bill McLaughlin, *Asbury Park Press*; D.L. Stewart; William Ruehlmann, *Virginia Pilot*; Lynn Demarest, *Miami Herald*; Elena Jarius, *Colorado Springs Gazette Telegram*; Roger Worthington, *Chicago Tribune*; Bob Greene, *Chicago Tribune*; Jim Donnelly, *Burlington County Times*; Jeff Strichler, *Minneapolis Tribune*; Diane Hofsess, *Detroit News*; and finally, a real tip of my thanks to Park Elliott Dietz, MD, MPH, Ph.D., ODD, and Adm. Richard D. Milligan, USN, whose dedication got me into *Newsweek*, *Time*, *The New York Times*, and countless additional media exposure.

Thanks again . . . and where are you champs today?

MEDICAL

As karma goes, Christopher Eric Marlowe is a sweetheart. At least he's one of my good friends, one of the few independent and honest capitalists I admire. He's also become survival knowledgeable about the medical industry.

For example, when he was in the hospital recently, Eric put on an aide's smock and went to the colostomy ward, where he filled each bag with Jello.

Yet it was old Heffer who told me how to flunk a physical examination easily without taking drugs to do so. His stunt is great for raising the blood pressure. Wet down and suds up a bar of hand soap—Heffer recommends using Ivory specifically— then place it firmly under your armpit for 20 minutes prior to your medical examination. He says a tobacco-filled cloth bag, dipped in water, then placed under your armpit will accomplish the same thing. Even if the medics get suspicious and run blood, saliva, or urine tests, nothing will show.

One of my truly favorite friends is Barbara McNeil, the former model now splitting time between the medical and politico-baiting professions. In one of her school exams, a stuffy doctor asked her in a most pompous fashion what the difference was between an oral and a rectal thermometer. In her demure fashion she responded, "I would imagine, sir, it would be in the taste."

McNeil told me that the physician, Dr. Jonny Craig, was recently named as Head of the Joseph Mengele Medical Institute.

Diane Kohler, R.N., recalls from her nursing school days a truly evil instructor who really enjoyed making students' lives miserable. Diane offered many examples, then explained how they cured this evil witch, whom we could call Prof. Becky Bedpan.

"She had to have a hysterectomy and wanted that kept very quiet, even though she went to a local hospital because she could get it cheaper," Nurse Kohler recalls. "A bunch of us found out about it, and our entire class, about 60 student nurses, began to clip every coupon, every free product offer, everything and anything, related to tampons, panty liners, sanitary napkins. We sent in dozens of our own proof of purchase items . . . everything we could to have her flooded with similar products and information."

Nurse Kohler reports that the evil lady actually changed her ways, became nice, and, in true good spirit, donated all of the mail-order products to a local women's shelter.

Finally, here's one you can use with your own medic, even though it's a true story told to me by the Three Wise Ladies about when The Queen of the Amazons had to go to the company doc for a physical.

The doctor told The Queen, "I'm going to need a urine sample and a stool sample." Nodding her blonde bighair, she hoisted a leg, peeled off her panties, handed them to the astonished doc, and said, "Here you go, just what you asked for, and you'll find a variety of semen samples there, too, champ."

The reason these three titillating tarts remembered this is because it was one of the few times The Queen was wearing panties.

MEGGER

Bad breeding, bad chemicals, bad environment—who knows what makes some offspring become marks rather than being like the rest of us? I surely don't know, and neither does Ray Heffer, but Ray and I both know that most marks are like something a sick dog has shit off the edge of a deep cliff.

That's why Ray said he should have known better when he bought the major-purchase home appliance from a mistrustful salesmark, who later denied making warranty promises, of course. That's when Ray discovered a useful device known as a megger.

Heffer says, "A megger is a really useful way to 'smoke' major electrical appliances, e.g., refrigerators, washers, dryers, freezers. Electricians call this device a voltage generator, or, in jargon, a megger.

"It's a hand-cranked device available from industrial tool shops, electrical supply outlets, or you can rent them from large inventory rental shops. A megger can produce up to 1,000-volt output, which can fry most appliances, especially the capacitor on the starter motor."

Heffer says he attaches the AC line cord of the mark's appliance(s) to the megger and cranks away his frustrations, saying that the excess voltage he's introducing will not harm the main motor but will burn out the starting motor capacitor.

"These capacitors run about $20 to $30 each; added to a $25 to $50 service call and you're talking some serious payback for your mark," says Heffer.

In addition to his own appliance salesmark, Heffer told of a navy friend in Norfolk whose landlord ripped him off when he was forced to go along with George Bush's 1991 political diversion and oil war in the Persian Gulf. Heffer's friend used a borrowed megger in his apartment, in those of two other vacating folks, plus in the common laundry area to ensure that the landlord would be using more than the security deposit to get back on operational line.

MILITARY

One of my greatest memories of the military is rumors. When we were desperately short of water, ammunition, food, clothing, competent leadership, or even a visible enemy, we always had rumors to keep us going. And I often wonder today if it was rumor or truth that in the 1992 election, George Bush and Bill Clinton conspired to blame Ross Perot for the fall of the Roman Empire? And back in '92, why was Dan Quayle chanting "Three More Years! Three More Years!"?

When you gotta share close space with others, keeping relatively clean is relatively common military courtesy. Some folks forget to wash their hairy asses for weeks at a time. Navy vet Stacy Independence offered them a gentle reminder.

He recalls, "We were able to get fiberglass from our ship's piping systems. It came in little pads. Those of us who had to live in bays with a couple of literally smelly assholes sometimes would rub these fiberglass pads over the offending guy's rack. He got the message after five or six applications and a trip to the sick bay."

On the other hand, Stacy says some guys just start washing after the horrible itching starts, and the problem goes away for awhile. But, as he adds, there is lots of fiberglass on a large ship.

My favorite medic reminded me of a stunt guys used to pull on nasty drivers with their deuce and a half. There is a steel loop on each side door where you use a padlock to secure that door. The stunt is to put your own lock on the guy's door. He says it's a lot of fun . . . unless you're the driver and in a bad spot. Let your imagination do the walking, troop.

I'm sure you older vets remember DA Form 1341, the allotment form? Medic says this trick could land you in the slammer, so just laugh about it, don't do it.

He thought somebody might have pulled this stunt on some marks during Operation Shitstorm over in Saudi. Basically, it involves helping your mark out by allocating his pay for him by filling out a new DA 1341 with his signature and your imagination. But you had better know the system before you even think of laughing about this happening to some deserving mark. So says Michael Medic, and I always believe him.

Several guys wrote to report the use of dark black plastic toilet seats in military facilities. They suggested the use of Kiwi extra gloss on your mark's throne seat. See, black can be beautiful! I wonder if we could do the same thing on white plastic with that fancy drill team white? Ahhh, why not?

One unit in Germany had a typical beat 'em all up bully who loved to pick fights with weaker foes. One of my friends had a great stunt to welcome the bully to his new duty station when the battalion commander had him transferred before he was fragged.

"We also had a very disliked XO in one of the HQ

units, and I had his signature. So, I had an 'official' report typed about this bully being a drunk, a doper, and suspected of looking at little boys' genitilia. I 'signed' it with the unpopular XO by tracing via a window pane," my friend reported.

Through the justicevine, my friend heard that the bully had hassles from Day One and was transferred twice more, all with bad reports. Moral of story: Don't fuck with the machine's parts . . . real people are those parts.

Heffer remembers one stiff from basic training days, a reputed kiddie rapist. Payback was simple. Heffer says the guy slept nude with his prized possession proudly exposed. When the slime was asleep and his pole at early morning piss hard-on, some justice seekers lasso'd his member with one end of a long boot lace. They tied it somewhat snugly after they'd attached the other end of the line to one of his combat boots. Just after they all went their way that dark morning, someone tossed the guy's boot out the window.

Need to educate a REMF to the ways of "Sorry 'bout that"?

Nimrod had a friend of a friend of the company clerk who used to be allowed to lose leave papers for REMF assholes, especially losing them from the duty log. Done properly, this can spell that fun word AWOL.

The Donut Dollies can be made to help, too. Nimrod had a lady friend pose as a Red Cross official to inform a truly prick of a mark that his parents had died in a car accident. Immediate processing of emergency leave papers kept the mark from confirming the news. Remember that word? AWOL?

Both Nimrod and I recall a grand way to repay some ill-favor during inspection. I defer to Nimrod.

"Right before the inspection you simply introduce

food that you've smuggled from the chow hall into the mark's footlocker. You do this while he is distracted, usually burying it under clothes or at the bottom. Be sure it is covered, of course, and crudely."

$$$ Bill once promoted a mark by adding extra stripes to his uniform. He explains, "I squirted toothpaste into the inner sleeves of his field jacket. When he took off the jacket at the chow hall, he had these strange white stripes in addition to the issue ones. Hee, hee, hee . . . many questions."

The military conducts random searches of on-post vehicles for drugs, guns, peaceniks, etc. Maggie Mayday has used this policy as a preemptive strike against jerks. Simply plant the No-No Contraband of Choice in the mark's car . . . easier to do if he or she is a litterous person, when you can hide anything in the onboard trash. Then, do your duty—call and report. By the way, the term "litterous" is legit, a coinage of Ms. Millie Litsko, a Bell of PA semanticist.

You get those "I park anywhere" macho/macha pigs of all brass/stripes everywhere in the military. Chicken Man had a friend who was an MP. This base cop gave Chicken Man stacks of TOW IMMEDIATELY order stickers. These stickers trigger exactly what you'd imagine anytime they are spotted by any passing MP. The usual response time was less than 20 minutes on most military posts.

Chicken Man told me it usually cost the offending Mark about $30 to $70 to learn a lesson about parking where he or she should not do so, especially in handicapped zones.

One of my platoon sergeants loved to quote the classic European military authorities so we'd know that he'd done some reading. When teaching the absolute versatility of the basic bayonet (which is true, it is), he was fond of Napoleon's quote, "You can do most anything with a bayonet except sit on it."

One time, his colleague, Sgt. (at that time) George Hayduke followed that by roaring at the startled troops, "But, by God, that does not preclude you having some other poor sod perched on yours!"

What great memories that each year grow better and safer.

Of memories, humor, tears, and wonderful reading, I must recommend one of the finest, funniest, warmest, oddest, and most critical fiction books I have read about the Vietnam War. It is a combination of a combat diary, a drug-trip bible, and the classic *Catch 22*, written as a satire that bleeds truth on every page. WARNING: Revisionists, sensitives, PC police, and grown-ups will want to burn this book. If you've read this far, you'll want to read it.

This classic book, *1369*, is available from Halo Press, 902 West Second St., Little Rock, AR 72201. It was written by H. Lee Bell, a veteran USMC H-34 "dog driver" who captures what "it" was all about.

As my lifelong friend, The Good Colonel, told me in Panama many years ago about his war years in Vietnam, "I have been honored with active participation in the greatest balls up since Chamberlain believed Hitler."

MOTELS

M otel clerks are usually the most blasé animals on our planet. The average clerk will sign in and issue a key to a rabid, 9-foot grizzly bear armed with an Uzi and never once blink.

That's why Biggus Piraphicus was able to rent a motel conference room so easily and cheaply. He scheduled his totally unwitting mark into a room on a particular date and time to discuss a controversial local issue. In his fliers and advertising he made the mark out to be a rabid nut case and obviously chose a topic that would piss off a lot of locals. The payoff came when the local media became aware of this growing controversy and contacted that befuddled mark, who was starting to get truly nasty phone calls regarding a talk about which he knew nothing.

Repeat as required.

Dastardly Dan was hit with all sorts of hidden costs and taxes at a heavily advertised chain motel. Next trip through he registered under an alias, then loaded the shower head with powdered dye. Later, he had a locksmith friend duplicate the room key and several others over the next month of trips.

Using real letterhead as a master, he forged a letter of invitation for a free two-night "vacation" in the motel as a special offering from the chain. No confirmation or check-in required, "just treat the room like it was your own home, free, on us, for two nights." Enclosed with each letter was a copy of one of the room keys.

These were sent to friends for the first round, then to secondary marks for the second round after the motel knew something was going on. Dan reports a very high success rate.

A motel chain once irritated Tabasco enough that he got a screwdriver from his car and at 2 A.M. was busy at work removing, mixing up, then replacing the room number plates from random doors. He said it took him an hour to do 200 rooms all over the motel, with nary a witness. As nobody ever looks at a door number when they leave, can you imagine the confusion when the next set of guests checked in?

Piper Pub once had a friend who got a nasty disease from one of the hookers who used the nearby Rent-An-Hour Motel.

"I also had a mark that needed some big-time hassle. So, another friend from out of town rented a room there using this mark's name and address. Then we had the world's most horrible party there . . . trashed the place, shit on the floor and lights, hurled in the sink, shit and puked in the tub, imploded the TV tube . . . of course, we did that last, as we had the sound up real high to drown the other noise," Piper adds.

He said they thought about planting a woman's sleazy dress soaked in animal blood, but decided to do that the next time when they faked a murder for this mark. I'll keep you informed as to Piper's next actions.

When a zombie-clerk at another motel chain

wouldn't adjust VonHenry's bill to reflect a closed pool, closed coffee shop, and nonfunctioning air conditioning in August, our hero had ants help him achieve justice.

Ants love sugar, and VonHenry bought five pounds at a nearby market, then spent the next 30 minutes making sugar trails from the outside to each door room on the ground floor.

Ray Heffer rented a motel room with a fertile bathtub, i.e., there were "live things" growing inside the tub. For laughs, Heffer filled the tub with hot water and added ten boxes of Jello. He also thought of mixing lemon (yellow) and lime (green) in proportion to resemble urine to place in the toilet tank.

I recall being in a very modest hotel in our beloved Third World a few years ago on some business or other and asked the yawning clerk if at least the bed was clean . . . he was decidedly not.

His nose visibly leaking, he thought, then replied, "Yes, sort of, if you pick your spot carefully and lie very still in that one spot."

MUSIC

The Queen of Spades offers us her notes on making merry with music. She says to tape Slayer over your mark's favorite tapes. She says the singer sounds "like an unanesthetized cat getting reamed with a dentist's drill." You could also substitute many of the antiwhatever rap artists. Good God, what a horrible misuse of the word artist.

If your nerves have ever been assaulted by some cretin testing the upper limits of his amps and your patience, it's Chicken Man and his solder gun to your rescue.

"Do a little creative rewiring, like Tim Allen," says Chicken Man. "On my musical mark, I rewired to turn his amp and system crossover into a rectifier. Speakers can't hack DC current, of course, and the job I did on his set off the smoke detectors three floors away."

It was a simple cut and patch job using common Radio Shack stuff and a few minutes' time. *One note of caution:* Please be certain the amp is turned OFF before you begin your work. There's enough juice there to really kick you on your ass!

Speaking of doing the 60 hertz shuffle, Maggie Mayday offers some fun musical electronics advice for nontechnical folks. You can disable a deserving mark's stereo or boom box by replacing the fuses with open ones. You can use a single-edge razor blade or an X-ACTO knife to partially cut the drive belts for a tape deck or VCR. Foil runs can be sliced the same way.

Most IC chips are marked for position. Unplug and replug the wrong way. If a transistor won't fit in backward, snip off the offending leg so it will.

In a mobile unit, partially remove the legs so that the vehicle motion will interrupt contact, making that temper-tamping off/on sound.

Pencil lead conducts electricity. Draw circles around the key chips on circuit boards and transistors. Make sure at least one pencil line crosses a foil run on the circuit board.

Maggie Mayday also says you can easily short speakers by cutting the insulation off the wires and making sure they touch. If it's coax cable, stick a pin through it. Sound goes on, BOOM, all is smoked.

Here are some other simple but annoying stunts, also from Maggie. Lock the transport device on the mark's turntable or laser disc player. Change the voltage or hertz selector setting on any unit so equipped. Remove turntable needles; replace with nails. Cover VCR or audio deck heads with clear nail polish. Glob anything on a CD player's inner lens—shuts it right down. Change LEDs or bulbs to different colors. Reverse polarities. Remove key circuit boards. Heat CDs, LPs, videos, etc., enough to warp slightly. Maggie also superglues knobs, switches, and other setting devices to inappropriate levels. Rearrange cables, then glue the connections.

When Bummer and his band got nitpicked to quit

by a local bar owner who was underpaying and over-cheating them, the guys wrote a hilarious song about the man, his family, and his devious business practices, along with the unhealthy atmosphere in his bar's kitchen. They sang it to uproarious and hilarious reception in all of the other town bars.

And to them I add, anybody who fools around with the bandwagon is likely to get hit by a horn.

Recalling my use of those clever little musical-chip greeting cards, Steve Wilson suggested secreting an entire case of these little darlings surreptitiously about your mark's home, business, etc. Get really creative about how well you can hide them and how inconvenient you can make their removal. Steve tells me that in testing, he found these babies can make their noise for up to six days. Imagine all of that wonderful cacophony!

A group of do-gooders in an Up With People-type band had screwed over The Punisher as only the hypocritical God squad can do. He decided that some minor revenge was the key to scaling his attack appropriately.

"About a week before their next show, I created a self-published desktop poster design for them. I turned them into the worst sort of Up With Satan and Down With Christians nasty group. I tried to make them and their poster as offensive but as believable as possible," Punisher said.

He used lots of inverted stars, swastikas, and other signs of Satan. He made up new songs that the group would feature, "Screw Like the Beast," "Love Lord Lucifer," "Drugs & Hugs," "Put Crack in Your Lover's Crack," stuff like that.

The response was as expected, and the goody group hired a PI to find out who'd made the posters that were all over town. No luck. They went on local radio and TV to explain. There were still protests about them playing, and decency groups showed up, etc.

"Shit, I probably did them a publicity favor," Punisher said with an evil laugh.

Back in college The Butler was screwed over by Mr. Dirtbag, who also ran a band. Mr. Dirtbag took $500 cash from three frats to play a large combo party for them. He left for the semester, claiming to be terminally sick. He then stuck them for the money, as he said his band had broken up. He promised to repay when he got his medical expenses covered.

Neither The Butler nor I have much sympathy for fraternities, as many are simply an alcoholic pigsty of paid friends. But The Butler was owed another debt by Mr. Dirtbag and used music to collect.

Being a student journalist, The Butler had quiet access to the school newspaper and ran a small display ad twice the next week . . . after learning where Mr. Dirtbag had moved. Yes, the illness was a scam . . . he'd simply taken the loot, not paid the band members, and moved to an off-campus apartment. He had dropped out of school.

The ad read: "Mr. Dirtbag and His Band plays for frat parties. Now located at _____, Mr. Dirtbag will talk to you about playing frat parties. Call _____ for Mr. Dirtbag or just stop by in the evenings."

Not only was there a minor riot from frat rats invading Dirtbag's digs, there was an unexpected dividend. It seems Dirtbag had also been dealing drugs and had ripped off two suppliers who hadn't been able to find him. They showed up before the college boys. Eventually, the police were called.

This time, Dirtbag's medical and legal problems were very real.

NEIGHBORS

When you damage guard rails, road signs, and other public property during a car accident, the appropriate jurisdiction makes you pay for them. Squeamish had a drunken neighbor who used to frighten others by driving fast and poorly in the neighborhood while all boozed up.

"I collected wood, paint, and metal chips from some signs and posts that I knocked down with my sledge hammer late at night. I took all of this to the drunken mark's place and beat up the fender of his truck (it was parked 100 feet from his home) with my hammer," says Squeamish.

"Then I put the chips in the fender and stuck them into cracks and dents. I smeared yellow sign pole paint on the fender. Then I called the police from a pay phone and reported that a drunk had done a hit and run and almost run me off the road. I observed him turning into _____ Road. I also described his truck."

Big fine! Big costs! Big repair bills! Big fun!

Dastardly Dan had a hated neighbor who used to

shoot a bb gun at the little kids playing near his yard. One night, Dan and some friends hoisted a 300-pound cement block into the grump's yard, then tied a steel cable from it to his front door and hitched it tight. They did the same to the back door.

The guy tried to leave for work at 7 A.M., and it wasn't until 9 A.M. that the police arrived, then 10:30 until a tow truck came to rescue him. Dan and friends rolled on the floor of his home as they watched.

"Next time, and there will be a next time, we'll cut his phone line too," Dan added.

Dan's neighbor in another town was the nosy religious zealot who called the police if you washed your car without a shirt on . . . you were assaulting her. When she got a garage door opener, Dan learned the make and bought an identical-looking "key," which, of course, didn't have the same code.

"One night, I switched keys, putting the inoperable one in her car and taking hers. She opened the door from the inside, then got in her car and backed out. From across the street, using her key I closed the door on the roof of her car. She screamed and desperately began to push her 'key.' I opened and shut that door on her car roof six times in rapid succession, denting it badly."

And no, it was not some elderly battle ax. Dan says she was about 30 and totally obnoxious. The company replaced the system but charged her again, as they were able to prove she had the wrong key and they had the numbers for the one they'd sold her. She never suspected Dan and, indeed, complained to him about the problem and asked for his help.

"I told her this was God's will and that I wasn't getting involved."

Dan's wife's nasty ex-boss also lived in the neighborhood. Dan used to unscrew the guy's cable TV hookup outside the house just enough to break the connection. He'd do this on a weekend, then early Monday morning he'd tighten it again. The cable company would come out, check it all, demonstrate to Boss' wife that it was working, bill them, and leave. Dan would repeat the steps again and again.

The New Age Lady lived in an apartment neighbored on one side by some wicked aliens from the Middle East who used to steal her UPS packages, newspapers, anything not tied down. I guess this is cultural diversity. Being the great lady she is, Ms. New Age made up some parcels of her own, complete with authentic UPS labels. She put out the parcels; all were stolen. Her neighbors, all the spawn of camel humpers, smilingly denied everything, beamed and smiled some more.

The parcels all contained various containers of bodily fluids from several species in varying degrees of health and in varying degrees of spoilage.

Not only did New Age Lady's parcels stop disappearing, her neighbors stopped beaming and smiling, too.

When Kalamity wanted to snoop on her nasty neighbors in the next apartment, she simply had an electronics friend pay them a visit as a "utility inspector." He coordinated the frequency of their nursery monitor so that Kalamity could receive the signal, and he also quickly dropped another booster in the evil couple's bedroom. Kalamity had some interesting party tapes to leave around the complex laundryroom and entertainment center.

When Mischief Maker's neighbor tried to use his water system in her yard during the California drought, he was furious. She did it while he was away at work. Finally, he caught her at it. His response was to go over to her place at night and, using a 16-inch wrench, tightly

.shut off all her exterior spigots. He then poured a package of Round Up in her empty hose, went home, and shut off his water inside his house.

It took an expensive plumber to unwrench her spigots for her. And, as she couldn't use Mischief's water, she had to hook up her own hose. A lot of Round Up went out on that lawn . . . three days until desert time.

The Rubber Fox uses neighbors to get back at his mark. Using a city Cross Reference Directory, the Fox will locate someone in the neighborhood not real close to the mark, but "in the neighborhood," as they say.

The scam is that the Fox calls the neighbor about 3 A.M. posing as the mark. The conversation goes like this:

"Hi, this is _____, I know it's 3 A.M., but what the fuck, I can be neighborly. Me and the girlfriend are here sucking a few beers and thought you and the missus might like to join us, real neighborly like? We got some good porn tapes and my old lady here doesn't mind diddling another lady if you get my drift."

You may have to make four or five calls to get someone who is furious enough to call the police. If you're real lucky you'll get somebody who will take the mark up on the offer and show up.

It takes Mike from LA to finish off this set with a truly nasty and dangerous amusement, the results of which could be disastrous. It's called Any Kite In A Storm. Mike says to get to your mark's home just before an evening thunderstorm breaks. Locate the rooftop TV antenna and get up there as quietly as possible. Launch a kite, using fishline, as it is a conductor, and get that kite as much altitude as possible. Tie the other end all over the antenna and its tower, then leave quickly, quietly, and carefully.

As Tipper Beeweezel calls it, "lightning is God's deadly autograph."

OFFICES

Personalized memo forms and satirical adaptations of standard office forms have been with us since they were chiseled in stone. One of my favorites came from Claude Borfors, a journalist I knew in Central America back in the early 1980s. He says it truly upsets the tight-sphinctered among the office grown-ups.

If you want to piss off the humorless grown-ups in your office, you have my permission and that of Claude to reproduce the form on page 140 and use as many copies as you wish.

Next time you are truly bored at the office, stop, look around you, and study everyone. Smile, because everyone you work with is totally naked at least once a day. Think about that.

With the 1990s' economy the way it is, anyone can get a stupid minimum-wage job, even without a Ph.D. or technical degree. Renegade says you can use this fact by getting yourself a stupid minimum-wage job in your mark's name.

"Use your summer, your own vacation, or do it as a

TO _____

DATE _____ TIME _____ A.M.
P.M.

You are damn lucky to have me take your fucking messages.

M _____

OF _____
AREA CODE
AND EXCHANGE _____

TELEPHONED		PLEASE CALL	
CALLED TO SEE YOU		WILL CALL AGAIN	
WANTS TO SEE YOU		URGENT	
	RETURNED YOUR CALL		

MESSAGE _____

_____

_____

_____

OPERATOR

second job, but do it in your mark's name," says Renegade. "Fill out the application in his name, with his address. Use references who know the scam and are in on it. Of course it works; I've done it."

The fun is that you just don't give a shit. You can screw off (or on, if you like). Steal, fuck up orders, be rude to customers, be gross, vomit, expose yourself . . . it's all in your mark's name.

Enorap worked for a bitchboss who deserved to have the glass ceiling fall on her evil head. As she had a personality that would sour milk, Enorap thought it might be fun if other workers questioned the boss' personal hygiene.

He got a strong magnet and an empty, unwashed can of oil-packed tuna. He attached the can to the rearmost part of her metal desk, I think it's called the skirt, being certain that the attachment didn't impede drawer operations.

Enorap said it took less than a day for the rumors and looks to start. When she began to question, he removed the attachment so when she investigated her desk nothing was there. Several days later he attached a "fresh" can.

When Thrill Hammer was working for a Corporate Hydra's local office in Houston, his boss blamed two innocent employees for hawking phlegm on the men's room walls. He did so because they were union officers. They were also innocent. The guilty person was one of the office drunks, not a line employee.

Thrill Hammer says he took it upon himself and some trusted friends to bring Mr. Boss personally closer to phlegm. They spent a week hawking about a pint of the stuff into a jar. They gift wrapped it and put a touching card on it from Mr. Drunken Office Guy, the real villain. They had it delivered to Mrs. Boss, at home.

Fax machines have been a help to The Amityville Horror II, as she has used them to send very personal messages to ex-sweeties, co-workers, and others who

have harmed her. She says this works best in a profes
sional setting, especially with executives, and you're limited only by your erotic imagination and your budget . . .
unless you use Mark #2's fax.

Sometimes the mark will bring a bagged lunch to the
office and use the microwave for a reheat job. The
Cootie tells us that when you put an ordinary, soft
marshmallow into a microwave and heat for 50 to 70
seconds at high, those little snacklettes will swell up to
softball size. Imagine the effect from tossing three or four
of those cute little guys into your mark's lunch bag before it goes into the microwave for reheat, firing up to
high, and . . .

Jesse Vengeance had a good friend laid off by a boss
so the boss could give his bosomy niece a job . . . and
get close to her. Jesse and friend felt this sting, so they
repaid Mr. Boss. With a friendly secretary's help, they got
a duplicate of Mr. Boss' large briefcase. Before he was to
leave for a meeting, they filled it with a nest of baldfaced hornets.

We'll stop right here while I help him look for the
calamine lotion.

PAINT

Hair today, dye tomorrow, could be Saint Dan's battle cry as he used paint paranoia to have fun with a mark. St. Dan suggests finding a wall, car, window, or whatever that your mark considers to be sacred. Spray paint nasty graffiti on it, e.g., satanic or Nazi art, obscenities, etc.

Now, when the Mark discovers your artwork and thinks it's a costly clean-up job, the stunt kicks in. You've used new spray hair dye. Yup, hair coloring comes in cans, sprays on, and works just like paint. But it washes out much easier. Hence, mark spends Big Bucks to clean up what could have been done with a bit of water.

Dan's a saint.

Speaking of tainted advice, Bucko notes that all of the paintball ads stress that the paint is "washable." Bucko imagines removing the washable paint by hypodermic syringe and refilling with the hardcore paint of your choice.

A notice that came with my telephone bill recently told me to be careful when painting near a phone jack, as *paint can block a proper telephonic connection.* Gosh, can you imagine that, Ma Bell giving out Hayduke ideas.

Dr. Death had a nasty acquaintance to whom she wished to do a tad of colorful harm. She bought some luminescent paint, and in huge letters she sprayed the words CHILD MOLESTER on the front of the guy's house.

"The next day, old Sol activated the paint so that in the dark of the evening my message stood out like a neon light," Dr. Death related. "The local media showed up, and even though this vermin wasn't a molester, the media and the neighbors now have their doubts."

Fire where there's smoke, eh, Dr. Death?

PARANOIA

Mind games are best because we always win. Marks have weak, nervous minds, the perfectly fertile field to plant the quick-bearing seeds of paranoia.

Bigots of all persuasions fit easily into my crosshairs. Bigfoot Tom agrees and loves to "surgically" place specially edited cassette tapes at inappropriate opportunities. For example, he would substitute Richard Lester's 1976 tape "200 Years of Freedom . . . Red, White & Blue from a Black Point of View" or Richard Pryor's very hilariously rude "Is It Something I Said?" tape for a Louis Farrakhan meeting, a Jerry Falwell revival, a George Bush concert, or a Jessie Helms séance.

"The best deal is if you could get your substitute broadcast or played with minimal interruption," says Tom . . .

Silly putty, some wires, and other electronic gimmickry can create a perfect "car bomb" for your mark. Make it look real—lots of manuals out there on the real thing—smear it with a bit of grease and dirt, then have a friend "warn" your mark about a plot to blow his car all over town. Of course, this one should be the topper to a campaign that already set the stage. With luck, the mark will call the authorities. Let's thank free-lance terrorist Baka Scheisse for that laugher.

The Punisher has a Ph.D. in paranoia promotion. Not only did he endorse my initial idea a book ago, he has since come up with a better version. Plant a *real* bomb, but make *very* sure that something is glitched or unhooked. To make it look lethal but amateurish, Punisher says to fill a pipe with powdered ammonium nitrate (gee, right from my old Company manual), seal, and set. BE CAREFUL!!

You gotta have a fried brain pan to like this one, which is why I'm still laughing. It's from Krazed Kaliko and involves potatoes.

Get a good head/shoulders photo of your mark. Get it enlarged to 4x6 and cut away all of the background from the head. Using glue, carefully paste the head on the back of a popsycle stick. Then, stick the other end of the stick into a potato, leaving just enough showing as a "neck."

Insert a sharp stick in the other end and "plant" these in the mark's lawn, office, apartment, or wherever it will do the worse good. Plant a whole crop of these Mr. Mark Potatoheads.

This is so ridiculous and foolish that it will work. I mean, whadda you gonna tell the police, Mr. Potatohead Mark?

Krazy also suggested sending rotted spuds, each enclosed in a little pine coffin, to your mark. As anyone who's smelled both knows, a rotting potato smells just like a mini version of a decomposing human body.

It's rotten, but Rev. Gene says that mail coming to your mark from the North American Man/Boy Love Association could create some problems. Or, it could open an entire new avenue of social life for your mark. Either way, you'll win in the end.

Both Rev. Gene and Sister Mary Wailingwall told me about The Stare as a weapon of body language. You simply stare at your mark. The good Reverend had a nasty landlady who used to snoop. So, then, did he. He would snoop up behind her when she was watching TV at night, stand, and stare at her until what had been passed as her brain registered his ghostly presence. She'd jump, startled, and demand to know what he was doing. He would continue his staring until she repeated the question, then simply smile and walk away.

Thrill Hammer worked for a very fundamentalist religious puke who constantly harangued all employees to "get on God's team," then began to demand that they volunteer 10 percent of their subsoil-level nonjob wages to his church via extra "tithing."

First, Hammer put some mercaptan on the gas pipes coming into the shop, which made the nervous boss call out the fire department. They billed his ass for a false alarm. Then, Hammer changed the stick-on lettering on the man's home mailbox to Mr. I.M. SATAN, #666.

Hammer got a couple of other employees to knowingly wink at Mr. Religiousboss at least a dozen times a day . . . very unsettling to him. Hammer's finale: repeat all of the above.

A similarly religious buttdrop had given the Queen of Spades a tough time. She liberated two of those old cow skulls that folks in the western U.S. use in landscaping. She painted a red pentagram on the forehead of one and an inverted cross on the other. She hung them on the mark's door and from his front yard lamp post while he was away for a week.

"Many, many folks drove by that jerk's yard and saw

the evidence that he was marked by Satan. During the week, at night, I would come by quietly and smear animal blood on his driveway and on his home," Ms. Spade reported.

The Dark Master's neighbor was a chickenhawk, an all gung-ho Rambo who always had an excuse never to go for real. This turd also flew a large American flag from a 70-foot pole in his yard, all day and night.

"That's not proper respect for our flag," Dark Master claimed. "So one night I hauled down his flag and disposed of it according to the manual. I replaced it with a Nazi battle flag. I also put hose clamps around the flag ropes so he couldn't haul it down easily."

Sounds like a FUBAR (ask a vet) to me. Dark Master said the guy had to rent a cherry picker from the local power company to get the Nazi flag down. The local media covered the event, as did the local Professional Jewish Advocates, who reported Mr. Mark to the authorities. This took place in Pennsylvania, which has heavy-duty antihate laws against ethic intimidation.

Way to go, Dark Master. And, as the former Associated Press guy Terry Anderson once said in Beirut, "Shiite happens."

PARKING LOTS

As Steven Wright asks, why do we park in driveways and drive on parkways?

The parking lot owner swore absolutely that nobody had damaged Mike R.'s car while it was in *his* lot. He smirkingly told Mike to sue him.

Instead, Mike came back very early one morning before the lot was to be opened. Mike went to the exit lane, where a large sign said DANGER . . . DO NOT BACK UP . . . SEVERE TIRE DAMAGE BY SPIKES!

He removed the steel cover plate and used a ratchet wrench to loosen the spikes' connecting rod. He then turned the rod the other way so the spikes were facing the departing traffic.

Mike R. thought it might be fun to be around when the first four or five motorists exited the lot that day. But he didn't. He just thought about it.

Chicken Man wanted to help his community clean up its roadways. He also knew a parking lot/tow pound service that he needed to pay back for some expensive and unjustified evil it'd caused him.

"I knew this cheat charged $75 per tow and $20 per day storage. So I drove around town and spotted six or seven cars that were just sitting along various roadways. I called the tow guy and ID'd myself as the owner of three cars and had a gal friend do the same for the rest. We told him we needed a tow to his place, as the cars were broken down," says Chicken Man.

Apparently, it worked all too well, as the tow lot operator spent much of the next 10 days explaining to police why he'd towed cars illegally. Apparently, the signs of incoming dollars were larger than his peanut brain.

License plates have always fascinated me. Nimrod has some fascination with them, too. He also had a parking lot owner he wanted for payback. Nimrod says that a parking lot is a mammoth collection of license plates just waiting for creative editing.

He says, "A little tape, colored the same as the plate background, does great editing for you. With a small snippet of tape, an O becomes a C, an E can become an F or an L, a B can be an 8 or a 3, and so on. With a little planning you can have a lot of fun in a parking lot, changing plate numbers without changing plates."

Perhaps it's not the lot or owner upon which you want revenge. Perhaps your mark just parks his or her car there. Harry Leadballs mixed some green food dye with water and poured it under the radiator of his mark's car. He also puts candles into the tailpipes to get that great smoky effect, and a balloon over the end of the pipe makes a great superfart sound when it pops.

But, Super Dave had the wonderfully gross-gross idea. He removed the backseat of his mark's car and took a dump on the floor, then put the seat back. A Phi Beta Kappa from Excrement U, Super Dave says the guy looked everywhere but under that seat . . . even tore up his car's air conditioner.

PLANTS

Flowers are interesting creatures. As Richard Iannelli points out, flowers are "one of nature's most exquisite things of beauty, which few people take the time to appreciate fully while they are alive and yet which, peculiarly, most people have surrounding their coffins . . . when they can no longer see or smell them."

And, as the members of the Ladies Green Thumb Garden and Vocal Marching Society have pointed out, plants also have uses as well. For example, Nancy, Elaine, Lucy, and Gretchen told me how they were itching to use *ichunga* on two enemies, the evil Dick and David.

For you non-hores (jargon for horticulturalist), *ichunga* is a small, prickery South American plant that gives you a painful chemical-contact sting that will last for an hour.

Closer to home, Pepper suggests carefully harvesting, then boiling down poison ivy leaves *in the open air* (don't breath in the steam). Then anoint the clothing or body parts of your mark with the resultant concentrated magic potion. Pepper says this is only for the truly deserving.

We've mentioned Ortho's Triox before, and JimJam writes in to tell us that he has "personally supervised its use in a truly just and environmentally sound manner, and it's fuckin' awesome."

So, if you're up for totally destroying your mark's entire lawn, Heffer, that loyal old salt from Kansas City, says to spread road salt liberally on the targeted lawn. Krazy Kaliko adds that it helps to do this before a light rain or at night so the dew soaks it in well.

Oliver Shitmuckle, a friend of Jason Campos, had a mark who refused to pay Oliver what he was owed for some lawn work. Oliver waited a season, then when Mark went on vacation, Oliver and a helper scattered several hundred pounds of Rice Crispies cereal on the guy's lawn. It took five weeks to clean up the mess.

In a similar sense, Pyro tells us that passion fruit, blackberry, and trumpet creeper are fun to plant on your mark's lawn whilst said mark is away for a couple of weeks. According to Pyro, these are very invasive plants and almost impossible to get rid of once started. The Butler has since added kudzu to this list.

Also, Dr. Frankenswine planted three dozen packages of rutabaga seeds in a mark's lawn a few years ago, noting it was a bumper crop in all disrespects . . . drove mark into a vegetative state.

And, to coin a phrase, let's end on an upbeat change with the advice from Laurence Coster, who says that quarters fit very snugly in the end of most garden hoses.

In our fun business, having a black thumb is not necessarily wrong.

POLICE

Here's a great story from a fine-humored Canadian police friend, John Subgun. Actually, John's story is about a stunt that was done solely as a practical joke. It frightens me to think what John and his chaps might do if they actually got serious about a mark.

"We managed to lift the target's wallet in such a way that he thought he'd misplaced it in the office or at home, so he didn't say anything to us about it," John told me over a few lemonades at the Sink Homestead, located just a stone's throw from the Croup Stained Glass Studio. "He was a very serious, very married officer, and we let him stew until he went out on his patrol tour alone for eight hours.

"When he returned from his tour, one of the senior officers sent for the poor guy, ordering him to report to the command office.

"He reported in and saw his wallet on the boss' desk. The senior officer looked very haggard and serious. He asked the poor chap if this was his wallet and made him identify it twice, then shook his head.

"The poor fellow was baffled and asked in a nervous voice what was wrong. The senior officer looked him straight in the eye and told him that his wallet had been found that same evening, next to a dead prostitute . . . how did he explain that?"

So, John, how did he explain it? According to John, he didn't. He fainted. When he was revived he was let in on the joke, yet for some reason was not as amused as his colleagues.

Nathan sharpened his blade of humor on a nasty chap who stiffed him on a loan. Since he'd pinched Nathan's funds, Nathan pinched his mark's wallet . . . the safe way.

"I went to a discount store and bought a cheapie wallet, which I loaded with some cleverly created ID that 'belonged' to the mark. I stuck a couple of bucks in there, then proceeded to do one of those single-digit IQ stunts like a B/E on a 24-hour convenience store, being sure I'd tripped the alarm.

"While fleeing I dropped my mark's 'new' wallet in the back of the store. Of course, if you can obtain the mark's real wallet it makes the case tighter, especially if he or she has no real alibi. Using the law to help civilize a stupid or nasty mark is always a step in the right direction," Nathan added.

Speaking of which, were you aware of what they've named the neighborhood crime watch program in Siberia? It's called Watch Your Steppe.

Thanks to Rev. Nastyman's diligent research, as noted in that learned tome, *The Quarterly Journal of Dust*, Dr. Hace Polvo, editor, here are some Truths You Must Recognize When Being Dealt With By The Criminal Justice System and Its Minions. See if any of these sound familiar:

- If you've done nothing wrong, you have nothing to fear.
- If you're innocent, we'll have you out of here in no time.
- I'm only doing my job; it's nothing personal.
- I'm here to protect your rights, too.
- Make it easier for all of us; talk to me before the lawyers get here.
- We only want to talk to you, so please open the door.
- Plead to all of this and we'll get you probation.

ICBM suggested a fine use of his desktop publishing setup to help local merchants in their battle against the parking police. Our helpful capitalist says, "I print hundreds of OUT OF ORDER stickers and hang them on parking meters in the early morning hours before our town opens."

Finally, I remember the last public words of John Edgar Hoover, who wheezed, "In God we trust; all others we monitor."

John's actual last words were known probably only to Clyde, and they may not have been words. Love's like that.

POLITICS

I had to go to the District of Columbia on business the other day, and I always feel as if I'm in a foreign world when I step off the airplane at Washington National. I begin to sweat and reach for my passport. One amusing thing happened, though. I stopped in a men's room to offload the Diet Poopsi that USAir had snacked me with when I noticed a graffito under the hot-air hand drying machine. It read: PUSH THIS BUTTON FOR A MESSAGE FROM YOUR CONGRESSMAN.

Their major message is, of course, "In nonsense there is unity."

Come back Tim Wirth . . . we need you!!

Anyway, Jon Ford, of editing, imbibing, and trolling fame, told me a wonderful stunt that happened in a local election back East. It seems Candidate Shyster, an incumbent prevaricator, had scheduled one of those half-hour commercials to lie to the voters. The incumbent was one of those slick-as-a-Vaseline-enema types.

Meanwhile, candidate Challenger, our kind of guy, purchased three minutes of TV time on the same station immediately prior to Shyster's talk. His message consisted of a truly ugly test pattern accompanied by a horribly shrill, ear-ripping whistle. Obviously, a lot of would-be voters switched to another channel.

If voting made any positive changes in our country, the politicians would make it illegal. President Clinton and her husband continue to sodomize our civil rights with their tooth-fairy agenda, just as their two predecessors did with their greed agenda. After 12 years of Reagan/Bush, though, it is a change to have a president who doesn't think Aretha is a bladder disorder.

Vote often! Biggus says in states that allow you to register by mail, you can file a change of address card for your mark via the voter registration office. That way you will have helped your mark be registered twice. Wait until some bureaucrat in a fiberglass suit and the personality of a demented wolverine stumbles across that no-no.

In a similar sense, Jake the Ox suggests that you switch party registration for your mark. Be creative with this one.

Savage Henry's mark was a local politician in a rural area. Henry had bogus campaign posters printed for his mark, which he put up at night after ripping down the opponent's signs and littering with them. Mr. Mark got blamed. Henry did it again, only this time he put the opponent's signs in a garbage bag, which he stuffed in the mark's Dumpster. He called the opponent to report this. Nobody believed the mark's innocence, and he lost the election.

Well, it's time to quit, as I see that primary election time is almost upon us, time for those sleazy politicians to change their skins. I am convinced that these reptilians would steal the condom off a man during the act of intercourse.

PORNOGRAPHY

According to publicist Marlene Cleftcricket, the American Family Association will soon publish that group's own version of "Roots." It will be called "Weeds." Where is the Triox when and where we need it most?

Speaking of unrequited needs, where are the balls of the American entertainment industries and sponsors who are afraid to tell Don Wildmon and his AFA fascists to commit a physically impossible act of procreation?

Must we little folks do all of your First Amendment support? Consider that to create some discomfort for a former Jesse Helms aide, the famed artist Momzer Huaqueros created a violently graphic work of true pornography and surreptitiously hung same in a city museum, putting the Helms' aide/mark's name and unlisted home phone on the donation plaque.

Ms. Anon was academically sucker-punched by her mark, an ancient, dirty-minded professor who hit on Ms. Anon and was told politely to back off. The second and third times were less polite. Bad moves, because the fourth hit brought out her talent for destroying puckerbrains.

Using the professor's real name as a penname, Ms. Anon wrote a highly personal, erotic homosexual poem called "The Slow Spark of High-Heeled Boys" for the state poetry society's monthly booklet. Ms. Anon tells me it was "great chicken-hawk stuff about a doe-eyed boy bitch in tight Guess jeans."

Since then, there has been much huffing and charge hurling among members of the state poetry group, with the professor embattled on all sides. Because he is a shit and unpopular, few accept his denials and disbelief.

The Rubber Fox had a local and powerful business type screw him on a business deal, then laugh to his rich friends about it. The old Fox went to a publish-it-yourself print shop and created a flier that said something like this: WANTED . . . BOYS AND GIRLS BETWEEN AGES 9 AND 12 FOR PERSONAL, ROMANTIC PHOTO AND VIDEO ACTION SESSIONS. He used the mark's name and home phone on it. The Fox made hundreds of copies and posted them in town.

"I also stuffed some inside of newspapers at convenience stores. He got lots of threatening calls, two police visits, and some suit types in a state car finally arrested him," The Fox said with a chuckle.

As all vets know, there is a lot of sexual harassment and bullying in the military. Most is still condoned because the Brotherhood of the Military is the largest jock fraternity in the world. That's why I laughed at The Blow Queen's letter.

As a loyal member of the military, she knows of what she writes . . . sexual hassles. If she can't handle it with tact or threat, The Blow Queen usually writes a letter to the post's commanding officer or the military police's top cop or to the nearby local civilian mayor.

Posing as the mark, who is always a guy, the Blow

Queen writes a matter-of-fact, kind of blasé letter that "he" gives great blow jobs, a skill he learned while in the military. He offers to give the reader the best blow job of his life just for fun.

"It's worked each time and every time," The Blow Queen notes. "The turd who wouldn't leave me alone always gets his ass in a sling over 'his' letter. Sure, his lack of guilt or their lack of proof will surface after awhile. But the rumors and reputation live on."

In the meantime, I was just listening to Rush Limbaugh—what a fuckin' funny entertainer that bullshitter is—and heard that the nation's leading manufacturer of vibrators is Genital Electric.

Rush Limbaugh. To me he seems to be the sort of guy who would applaud some DAR member who could fart the national anthem if he could (A) take credit for it himself, and (B) make a fast buck. I love that guy . . . he's P.T. Barnum with brains.

Q-TIPS

Ever hear of the word *gentrea*? That's the small area of a car's windshield beneath the steering wheel used by tiny, elderly drivers. It's the only place they can see out. Dick Croup calls those folks Q-Tips. If you've ever been stuck behind one of those elderly condo commandos driving 4 miles per hour in Florida, you'll know exactly what he's talking about.

Perhaps, as Mischief Maker suggests, we should deny these folks the use of the road. Mischief says that needle-nosed vice grips do a grand job of clamping off radiator, fuel, and power steering hoses, just to mention a few. Or a U-type muffler clamp will put a shock absorber out of business.

Although Q-Tips will rarely use turn signals, they are big with the horns and lights. As Dennis Martin points out, you could help a Q-Tip by splicing together the wiring for the horn and lights. As Dennis says, "That way they have to deal only with one function for both thrills."

On the positive side, Grey McGeary says that plastic Bingo chips, commonly used by condo commandos in

Florida, will work well in pay phones and parking meters. He says to insert a real coin last if the metering device has a viewing window.

Perhaps sticking up for Q-Tips, Marty Kung tells of defeating tailgaters by bolting two extra horns under his back bumper. That way, when he's tailgated or has a horn beeped at him, he lets his car talk back.

Speaking of geriatrics, Stella asked me if I knew how to get three little old ladies to say "fuck." Shocked at the thought, I shook my head appropriately. She replied, "Have a fourth little old lady scream 'BINGO!'"

Stella and her sister in crime, Ruby Mucous Farkas, were visiting a geriatrically enhanced terminal storage facility—that's PCese jargon for old fogies home—over the holidays. They told me that the favored leisure-time game there, next to open-mouthed naps, is a brisk round of bobbing for dentures.

"Each guest removes his or her dentures and they all toss 'em in a toilet bowl, then they all just bob for dentures," Stella reported.

The stunt here, of course, is to use these stories to either frighten elderly marks or to be sure that younger marks don't become elderly ones.

Be careful out there. One of the leading causes of death among the elderly is dying.

QUICKY PISS-OFFS

Eugene Mormon and I were discussing our usual philosophic meanderings about life, hypocrisy, and that sometimes the bars of life ought to be reversed. I was probably feeling sorry for myself when Eugene rallied with a rousing, "PUT UP YOUR HAY-DUKES!" I laughed.

I also laughed when Lia O'Leary, a luscious lassy with an evil twinkle, suggested something we agreed to call "Quicky Piss-Offs." Lia, a young friend with a thoroughly wonderful mind, suggests that sometimes you just want to do something nasty to someone because he or she has irritated you a little, not enough for a full-blown payback.

I think you'll quickly catch Lia's intentions here when you read through some of her quicky piss-offs. Happy urinating on your mark, in a figurative sense, of course.

Lia says that you can piss off:
- a female by leaving the toilet seat up and not flushing
- anyone by using the last bit of toilet paper and hiding the replacement

- a semienemy by "borrowing" his/her fine book and dog-earring a dozen pages
- the elderly who drive 10 MPH in the fast lane with a perpetually lighted turn signal by tailgating them relentlessly
- a crossword puzzle addict by finishing his/her puzzle in ink . . . and incorrectly
- a roommate by peeing heavily all around her/his bed just before wake-up
- a VCR movie pirate by rerecording over the best tapes in his/her collection
- lost drivers by giving them directions that leave out a few key turns
- visitors, patrons, or guests by either stealing or vandalizing their umbrellas during a big storm
- dinner guests by talking forcefully enough with your mouth full that food falls out, ignoring the debris, or cleaning and paring your fingernails or teeth with another guest's silverware
- colleagues, roommates, or whomever by pretending to take phone messages but not doing so; lie when asked about it
- classmates or friends by randomly highlighting others' books with no reason or pattern
- anyone with dignity at a wedding or funeral if you goose or honk the holy man's johnson, or fart loudly, then turn around in your pew and laugh, urging applause, a trick Lia learned from Hilda

A couple more folks with quick piss-offs include Ms. M.J. Berg-Hyphen-Heiser, who sits back with amused delight after uncapping other people's toothpaste, then wetting their brush. Elaine, the FSU Crackerhawk, finally got her pal Merle to build a Superclicker so that she can override the normal TV clickers that men use to control

TV viewing. Clickers are the male sexual wands of the 1990s, or so says Elaine.

And so it goes. We'll have more of these quick piss-offs in future books. If you have some you'd like to suggest, send them along so Lia and I can judge them for inclusion.

QUOTES

As I do in each of my books, I am including wonderfully fine and funny quotes that are available for you to use in your life.

These quotes make fine philosophy for your own peace of mind, are creative thoughts to muse upon, or can be used as graffiti or custom bumper stickers. They also make great lines to spice your conversation.

"Through this world I've traveled I've seen lots of funny men. Some will rob you with a six gun, some with a fountain pen."
—Woody Guthrie, "Pretty Boy Floyd"

"The mashed potatoes of righteousness have no lumps."
—The Rev. Francis Dolarhyde

"A bit of voyeurism in the defense of liberty is quite nice."

—William Vincent

"God hates the homeless, too."
—Republican National Committee/1992

"I'm like a porcupine; leave me alone to climb trees and chew bark and I'll never bother you. Get me mad, though, and I'll load your fuckface with quills."
—Charlie Willsey, courtesy of friend Tom

"I am always ready to learn. I'm just not always ready to be taught."
—Winston Churchill

"A man's greatest joy in life is to break his enemies and to take from them all of the things that have been theirs."
—Genghis Khan

"Our sense of revenge is as exact as our mathematical faculty, and until both terms of the equation are satisfied we cannot get over the sense of something left undone."
—Inazo Nitobe, *Bushido*

"Now don't you two go out and get all blotto."
—Jane McGeary, Mt. Kisco, NY

"I don't blame the Japanese for buying up our country. I blame the assholes who put out the For Sale sign."
—Bob Goldthwait

"Venom knows no statute of limitations."
—Aunt Nancy, Cabo San Lucas

REMAILING SERVICE

As a chameleon, or, more accurately, an anaole, changes its hue for various reasons, we sometimes require that our marks receive mail posted from some locale other than our own turf. Many commercial remailing services advertise. But none has won the coveted Jon Kreig Seal of Creative Haydukery. That honor goes to a wonderful Australian lady named Barbara, who is more than the world's best remailer, she's also a grand friend of mine.

Barb's standard, nonprofit fee to remail your missives from Australia is $5 (American funds, please) in cash. That gets you a standard business-sized letter sent anywhere in the world via airmail and bearing that great, colorful, and official Aussie sticker.

Barb tells me, "I know from empirical observation that strange mail received from foreign lands makes many marks very jittery. Plus, it's also impossible to trace back to an original source this way."

She says that you should not put your mark's letter in any preaddressed U.S. or Canadian envelope. Just put whatever you want her to remail for you in a plain white envelope, plus give her the name and address of your mark. Put all of this and the $5 in an outer envelope and air post it to:

Barbara McNeill
14 Verdon St.
Williamstown 3016
Victoria AUSTRALIA

RESTAURANTS

Used to be when you went out to eat you expected great food and true service. Today, you hope for fast mediocre but expect the wurst. The demise started when food capitalists learned that fast beat good. Hell, most of our good citizens would eat deep-fried hog sphincters if they could get 'em quick and the place offered coupons.

Speaking of fast-food places, Jeff Charles of WJNO introduced me to Duane, his brother Jeff, plus friend Pam. They were all fired by the teenpimple manager who ran the local Eat & Puke. The manager then hired his asshole buddies.

Duane said, "We set a perfect alibi with an understanding parent, then got into the place after hours with a friend's help. We put a dead dog in the orange drink mixer that was out in the eating area and left."

The next morning the place opened for the lunch crowd, and the drink machine was turned on. It was fully 10 minutes until a customer spotted the dead dog revolving around in the drink tank. She screamed big time.

Even pandemonium went wild, followed by a major clusterfuck. All of this was followed by a major investigation (Duane and Jeff had tipped health officials), after which the teenmaggot manager was fired.

The Renegade had a major payback for a fast food outfit that had really messed up his sister's life for awhile. He did it by getting other customers angry with the outfit.

"I pulled up to their drive-through microphone and made sure there were about six or seven cars behind me. I'd give a fairly large order, then drive totally away," Renegade reported.

The result is that the person behind Renegade got Renegade's order, while the person behind that one got the next order, and so on. He and several friends did this in random fashion for about four months.

Cruising right along, I recall one winter when Chuck Goode did a tour as a waiter on a large tour ship. He had one truly bitchy lady who gave him all sorts of grief, no tips, and even hassled him when she was not in his station (serving area). Sympathetic kitchen staff offered to help by building a special danish for the lady.

Chuck told me, "I won't say what all was in there, but some of the ingredients were body functions, including a booger topping. She loved it, ate every bite."

He should have asked her if she wanted him to butter her muffin. Or is that inappropriate? And what if he had suggested the lower-caloried spread instead of butter? Oh well, perhaps this next idea will sound better.

Some customers get tired of facing the music. Bothered to distraction by strolling fiddlers hoping for a major tip, The Chancellor, always an astute man with a buck, simply deducted a "listener's fee" from his dinner bill. Startled management accepted this.

Ryan Haskell had to pay back another fast-food

place. Seated in the back of the joint, he stood on the table and carefully loaded two pounds of flour on the wide blades of the ceiling fan. Next, he broke the filter out of a cigarette and replaced it with a small firecracker. He lit the cigarette, left it smoking in the ashtray at his table, and left.

Watching from the parking lot he heard the firecracker explode and saw the hassle and the customer freakout. The manager came running and turned on the ceiling fan to clear the air. Amen.

From flour to floor, I was in a restaurant so greasy that the cockroaches had to wear cleats just to get around. It must have been that way for Darren Ankenman, who told me about his friend who rewarded dirty restaurants by stuffing dead roaches and other objects into condiment containers for other customers to discover and complain about.

Well, all of this has made me hungry, so it's time to go power down some manly doses of animal fat. The moral of which is, if your shit floats, there is too much fat in your diet.

SEX

A duck walks into a sex boutique and asks for a package of Ford's Finest Tickler Condoms. Saleslady coos, "Those cost three dollars each. Shall I put that on your bill?"

Duck says, "Sorry, I don't do oral sex."

Ray Heffer had a least favorite mark at work. He found the mark's picture in the company magazine, carefully cut it out, and mounted it on stiff cardboard. Then he rolled a condom over it, tied a knot, and dropped it in the management suggestion box.

"You could easily identify the mark through the thin rubber," Heffer added.

A similar stunt was done by Philboyd Studge, who got a portrait photo of his markess, carefully cut out her head, and rubber cemented it at the top of a condom as if she were wearing the condom as a dress. He rephotographed this extraordinary spectacle and had dozens of postal cards printed for present and future dissemination.

George McGeary once placed a phony sperm bank donor ad for his mark with outstandingly embarrassing results for the mark and his family.

An obnoxious apartment neighbor used to annoy Georgia Peach and her friends with his lewd comments and sexual invitations. Georgia and a friend finally tired of saying no to this crawlie creep, so they cooked up this deal where they'd both give him a body massage at his place.

"We sure did," says Georgia. "We were in bikinis and made him keep his underpants on while we lathered him all up, including his hair. We'd mixed Nair with perfume into our oil and really lathered him all over, including on his pubes.

"We told him to go get a shower and we'd meet him in his bed, naked. As soon as he hit the shower, we hit the door and never looked back. He never spoke to us again . . . after coming back from a two-week 'business trip.'"

Rev. Eugene had a friend whose spouse played around. The friend found out where the playground was and decided to shock the lusting couple as they did the lustful deed.

"He put a fine steel screening under the bottom sheet but over the mattress so that it was not visible or feelable. He then attached the zip cord and plug, then set a timer for the induced static to replace the action about halfway through," Rev. Eugene told me, adding that it worked too well and burned the spouse a tad. And, if you've ever had your tad burned . . .

I've heard of cannibals woking their dogs, but Dr. Death tells me that some cobbers actually wank their dogs. Speaking of wanking, and who among us hasn't, would it disturb your mark to think that some inconsiderate wanker has spilled his seed all over the mark's car, desk, chair, bed, dinner plate, family portrait, clothing, date, spouse, or the urn containing old mummsy's eternal ashes?

Dr. Death's plan is to take a squeeze bottle filled

with one of the many formulae for artificial cum that I've shared via these books over the years, then squirt away. Dr. Death says a passable field formula is to mix mayonaise, Karo, soap scraps, and hot water together, blend, and let sit for 24 hours.

By the way, as one of the Idaho Olde Pharts told me, "You know you're getting really old when it takes you longer to recover from sex than to have it." On a more serious note, though, I would like to caution you to have safe sex. Remember, your good genetic line must be protected, i.e., don't marry outside your family unless all your cousins are gone.

SOURCES

Following are some annotated sources for materials, ideas, products, and persons which have proven to be helpful in the payback business. This is not a universe of sources, but merely a sampling provided by my experiences, the experiences of others, plus reputation among experts. My listing these sources does not constitute a Good Hayduking Seal of Approval; these are not endorsements or advertisements. Each listing was current at the time of publication.

However, as some companies move, go out of business, or stop communicating with the public, it is possible that you might not get what you want from these folks. You may not even hear back from them. My apologies. In the past, though, the folks I have listed have proven to be excellent sources. If any of you have sources of your own that you'd like to share with the rest of us, drop me a note: George Hayduke, P.O. Box 1307, Boulder, CO 80306.

Accuracy Systems, Inc.
15205 N. Cave Creek Rd.
Phoenix, AZ 85032

Wow, this catalog is a literary version of shopping in the special ops weapons room at Ft. Bragg. It's all here—weapons, munitions, commo—everything a Second World SF unit would have in its TOE.

Allied Publications
Drawer 5070
Glendale, AZ 85312

They list dozens of survival books and manuals that will have definite interest for you. They also sell maps of all sorts and descriptions. Some of their titles will frighten the grown-ups.

American Science & Surplus
601 Linden Pl.
Evanston, IL 60202

A gadgeteer's shopping mall between catalog covers best describes these folks. I've bought from them for years, for fun and for fun. They are honest, open, and sell quality goods at very fair prices. Their catalog is written by humans with a sense of humor, a rarity these days.

Anatomical Chart Company
8221 Kimball
Skokie, IL 60076

I was told this company supplies medical schools and students with charts and other anatomical products. I got one of their catalogs. It can easily supply your needs. If you have the money and a little imagination, you can get a lot of bizarre things from this catalog. Phew!

The Baird Company
1270 W. Markham
Perrs, CA 92571

Wonderfully stocked ID and mail order print shop featuring various ID for KKK, Nazi, Soviet, CIA, etc. Also, law enforcement products and individualized printing. Pittsburgh's Bad Rad says they have top-quality prices and service.

Black Knight Leathers
205 N. 45th St.
Harrisburg, PA 17111

Here's a great source for all sorts of kinky leather stuff: bondage straps, blinders, meat grinders, and so forth. They sell great stuff for revenge. Also, the owner offers a discount to buyers who mention this book.

Carolina Biological Supply Company
2700 York Rd.
Burlington, NC 27215

Should you need various insects for your school or other projects—including those large, ugly German cockroaches—these fine folks sell them.

Cloak & Dagger Publications
825-A 25th St.
Ogden, UT 84401

Interesting catalog of books, T-shirts, rubber stamps, letterheads, posters, videos gathered from and about the world's clandestine services. Neat products. I have bought from them.

Dallas Delivers
P.O. Box 64566
Dallas, TX 75206

This is a competent and cautious remailing service. I've had contact with the owner and am assured of prompt, private, and very discreet service. The charge is one dollar per letter.

Delta Press, Ltd.
716 Harrell St.
El Dorado, AR 71730

According to my pals in the book industry, these people are one of the most professional, efficient, and easy-to-do-business-with operations selling books these days. Their catalog is colorful, complete, and easy to use. The catalog itself is worth having; it's like a reference bibliography.

The Department of Unconventional Resources
P.O. Box 210352
Columbia, SC 29221

Run by someone called The Wiz, which is slang for Wizard and does not refer to a scatological function, this organization essentially puts into practice that which I put into print. I think they do this only on a harmless and theoretical basis, of course.

Factsheet Five
Mike Gunderloy
6 Arizona Ave.
Rensselaer, NY 12144-4502

Mike Gunderloy is a fine chap who has compiled an excellent, dependable set of references to the underground, independent publishing world. Users tell me each issue repays your modest subscription investment. I have seen and used copies of *Factsheet Five*, an invaluable reference tool to any Hayduker.

Fast Forward Express
P.O. Box 4609
St. Paul, MN 55104

Here are some broad-minded Midwestern folks who will process sexually explicit photos. They are very private, honest, and discreet. Write for brochure.

Gun Parts Corp.
P.O. Box 9
West Hurley, NY 12491

Mostly firearm parts and accessories, but they do have neat treachery stuff, too, e.g. portable noise makers, pyrotechnics, etc. Their catalog is a cheap $5 and is a very valuable reference book.

Horus Botanicals
HCR 82, Box 29
Salem, AR 72576

According to Dr. Deviant, these people sell exotic plant

seeds which grow into vegetables that give you creative and entertaining thoughts. It's all very legal, fun, and nifty, I am told.

Johnson Smith Company
4514 19th St. Ct. East
Bradenton, FL 34206-5500

They're back. And so what if they're not in Michigan like when we old duffers were kids. It's still the home of fake vomit, whoopee cushions, dribble glasses, and all the other fun stuff that teachers and mothers hate. They have a lot of other novelty stuff for the '90s, too. My copy sits in the crapper for toilet-time study. Al Bundy told me that he reads his JS catalog there, too.

Loompanics Unlimited
P.O. Box 1197
Port Townsend, WA 98368

This is one of the most useful, fun, and fascinating book businesses around. Michael Hoy is the proprietor and says his book catalog is for knowledge, joy, and pleasure. His catalog is like a library of books, all useful and enjoyable. Michael is a great guy, too. This is my favorite bookshop in the whole world, and that is the truth. Buy from Loompanics! The catalog alone is a magnificent source of rare and highly useful information.

Archie McPhee & Company
Box 30852
Seattle, WA 98103

They advertise remarkable bargains of the most curious

sort, and they're very much so. This is one of the most unusual and useful companies with which I do business. Their catalog is a trip in itself, hilarious and informative. For a few bucks, you can stock up enough fun stuff for three years worth of April Fool's days and 150 rainy days. A fun place!

New Mexico Cactus Research
P.O. Box 787
Belen, NM 87002
Highly recommended by Dr. Deviant, these folks sell various interesting vegetable and plant materials, including some exotic forms of cacti.

Nitro Pak Preparedness Center
133309 Rosecrans Ave.
Santa Fe Springs, CA 90670-4940
This is a survivalist's wish bookshop, with a good toss-in of health products and other "just in case" necessities. Dandruff recommends them highly.

Phoenix Systems, Inc.
P.O. Box 3339
Evergreen, CO 80439

These folks sell the real things that the pretender toy companies advertise in *Soldier of Fortune* clones. You can buy real pepper gas, glaser slugs, professional surveillance gear, locksmith equipment . . . *real* James Bond goodies. Be cool . . . they are.

Sargent-Sowell, Inc.
1185 108th St.
Grand Prairie, TX 75050

Your source for everything a municipal services department would need for a village or city . . . uniforms, gear, equipment, supplies. Best equipped cop shop I've seen, plus they're nice folks with whom to deal.

SCO Electronics, Inc.
581 W. Merrick Rd.
Valley Stream, NY 11580

I don't know these folks, but they did come highly recommended, and I've seen their catalog. They sell outstanding video equipment, including some very nonstandard stuff that Haydukers could use. They also sell other unusual and useful items.

Richard Sitz & Associates
P.O. Box 453
Cedarville, MI 49719

Their major product is a very, very useful report entitled *Telephone Secrets*. This report is filled with information that your local and long-distance telephone companies don't want you to know. For example, it shows you how to legally make Equal Access Codes work for you at no extra cost to you. The report is also a great money saver.

Dick Smegma
c/o P.O. Box 20923
Las Vegas, NV 89112-2923

This intelligent, experienced, and totally with-it disciple offers personal research services for folks who want to do books, articles, videos, or screenplays about topics germane to this book. His services are available on a commercial consulting basis and are limited to literary and cinematic efforts. If you want him to think up some kind of revenge scheme, first inform him that you are writing a book or movie script; then he'll be happy to assist you for a reasonable fee. NO ONE UNDER 18 YEARS OF AGE NEED WRITE HIM. And you *must* enclose a self-addressed stamped envelope for a reply.

Square Lake Enterprises
P.O. Box 3673
Logan, UT 84321

I've listed these guys for years, as they are good, honest people to do business with. They sell all sorts of highly useful "special effects" chemicals and other pyrotechnical paraphernalia. They are a good, safe source.

STINK

If your mom kept a spit cup on her ironing board and your dad liked to guzzle beer and listen to the police scanner while he watched the bug light, you probably grew up in a distinktive family, i.e., you farted openly at Sunday dinner with company at the table.

Thus we turn to Uncle Gerry and the late Rusty, pioneer members of the Flatus Hall of Fame, for some stinking good advice. Uncle Gerry tells us that jewelers use a compound called liver of sulphur to turn silver black. Activate it with a bit of water and it smells megatimes worse than any of Uncle Gerry's beer/sausage/sauerkraut farts. It's available at most serious hobby shops.

Other useful ingredients that smell like the decaying carcasses of large animals include butyric, caproic, capryllic, and caproanic acids. Uncle Gerry adds that his outstanding choice for a smell-alike of week-old vomit, dead goat, sweatsocks, bilgewater, and sick babyshit is n-butyraldehyde.

"It just won't quit stinking," Uncle Gerry claims. "A drop or two will last for several months and makes the air inside a warehouse unfit for humans."

His runner up is isovaleric acid, by the way.

Remember, this man is to flatulence odor what Henry Ford was to car manufacturing.

Chester Molester has created a stinker of an attack bomb. To release the charming aroma of HS, a bit of sulfur and a piece of candle wax will do. Heat the mixture until melted, then pour it on the heating coils of your mark's stove. The result will ruin everyone's appetite.

Another stink bomb delivery system is hurled our way by Doc Byte, who says to mix a half/half mixture of household ammonia and sulfur to your desired size of projectile. Use a funnel to put this mixture in a balloon, then add some air to the balloon to help bursting capability. Fire from a balloon launcher.

If your interest is stinking up a mark's interior environment without going to a lot of trouble, follow Ray Heffer's advice—use a propane torch. Buy the small model with a valve nozzle. Hide it where it will be tough to find, then barely crack the valve open, just so the gas seeps out.

After several days the odor will attach itself to most of the room's surfaces. Your mark's eyes will burn and s/he'll have a bad taste in yee olde mouth, Heffer says. No worries about fire or explosion, either, due to dissipation and room air. But there will be lots of irritation.

The Flying Hawaiian launches a grand scheme involving balloons, photocopies of $20 bills cut to size, and the worst scent of your choice.

His deal is to put the bogus money in the balloon, followed by the horrible scent. Next, without inhaling, inflate the balloon. Be sure that your mark(s) get the balloons. Perhaps it could be part of some scam promotion you could create. Through the thin, colored balloon rubber the photocopied (both sides!) money will look real. The mark(s) will burst the balloon.

Surprise!!

STUDENTS

Here's a positive thought from Paco Escobar. If your first-grade teacher was really old and really mean, chances are good that she's really good and dead by now.

If you have a truly confused twit of a teacher, Renegade says to hand in two assignments, yours and one in the name of some mark. How you do the fictional assignment is your decision. Do the same thing for quizzes. Try to get several other people to do this. It confuses muddled-thinking academics and can screw up some secondary marks, too.

When the Sperminator was in college, he knew several marks who used to cheat from his test papers or cut class, then bully notes from nerds. Sperminator used bureaucracy for payback.

"I got drop/add forms from a student worker friend, saved them a semester to deflect suspicion, then used my marks' Social Security numbers to add and drop them from classes with a stroke of a pen and/or a computer key. It always worked."

He also did a few grade-change stunts on people's transcripts.

It is very easy to do these things at most larger colleges, as they are incredibly poorly managed, with even worse internal security. Because they spend so much money on big-time sports and social entertainment for the grown-ups, they lack working budgets. Hence, most hire students to do mundane clerical chores. These students have access to computers and data. This tradecraft moment has been brought to you by Professor Maynard Clappsaddle, who went into teaching so he could experience the other side of the bell curve.

Speaking of contemporary college students, this bigshot drinker had worn out his welcome by puking all over his dorm floor again. CJ said they waited until he left to go get blind drunk the next night, which he did seven of seven nights. Then they went to work. As the dorm doors were inset into the walls with square corners, no molding, they used drywall to cover his door, spackled over the drywall, then painted it to match the wall color.

When the drunk came in much later, he spent two hours crawling up and down the hall babbling about his room. Some guys told him he was in the wrong dorm. After two more hours of being tossed from three more dorms, his "minder" convinced the groggy mark that the Dean of Students had caused his room to disappear and that he should call the dean immediately, it now being 5 A.M.

CJ leaves the conclusion of this delightful episode to your imagination.

Also tired of stepping in vomit and listening to drunken children, Morgan Beckman used a rope and gallon-sized plastic bag full of vomit, feces, animal entrails, and a nice trail mix combination variety for his revenge.

Morgan says, "I tied the rope securely around the full

bag, then found a window above the mark's. If his window is open, oh well, it's still OK. If it's closed, well, so much the better.

"With a good swing or two to build momentum, you send your gift smashing through his window and splattering into the room. It's quite a mess."

A student at the University of Bullshit, Bond 009's roomie was a complete waste. Worse, he partied in the room, cranked loud music, and had obnoxious friends. Bond 009's roomie was not interested in an education, whereas Bond 009 was.

To expedite roomie's departure, Bond forged a letter from roomie to the counseling center seeking help. He included all sorts of references to incest, suicide, Satan, and beastiality. Two days later the calls began from the counselors. As soon as roomie denied writing the letter, the personal visits began from the paid do-gooders. Within the week, mommy and daddy took roomie home.

Free at last, Bond 009.

BJ had a different problem, a hall monitor whose personality was that of a wasp sucking juice from a lemon. BJ says this jerk used to hide in people's closets to catch them drinking, masturbating, or, gasp, fornicating.

BJ says when they knew he was in one guy's dorm room closet, they snuck in the room quietly, quickly nailed shut the door, then left for the evening.

"We'd set this up by spreading disinformation about a party in this certain room, then made sure the occupant of the room had gone to a movie with friends so he'd have a good alibi. Eventually, some other residents heard the screaming, called maintenance, who pried off the door. Elapsed time . . . three hours," says BJ.

On another occasion, when the dork was out for the evening himself, BJ and friends got a passkey, opened his room, placed five live geese inside, locked the door, and left. You don't want to know.

One day the frat boys at one LSU kiddie care center bothered The Laughing Magician too much. He waited until their South Seas Party Night, a major drunkathon, to strike. The Magician spent much of that day gathering copious amounts of fire ants, which he later deposited generously in each brother's room along with a few Hershey kisses for food until the boys got to bed.

One of The Magician's allies started the rumor that the ugly red bites all over most of the boys were opening sores of a venereal disease.

With increasing financial pressures, universities are coming down hard on waste. For example, The Big Red Reaper reports that his school "sentences" students to from 5 to 20 hours of community service for smuggling, aka stealing, food from the cafeteria.

Big Red says to wait until your mark goes back to the dessert line, then smuggle some food into his or her book bag or coat. As you quickly leave, mention this to a monitor.

And, as cousin Andrew McGeary reminds us, at the University of _____, they've come up with a new use for sheep. Wool.

SUPERMARKETS

When Derrick Johnson was a stockboy for an Orange County (CA) supermarket, he and co-workers invented poultry bowling, which is just what it sounds like. It began as an efficient way to get frozen turkeys from storage to the display area . . . just slide 'em along the polished floor. Soon, it developed into a game, with two-liter plastic soft drink bottles as pins.

Obviously, this is not a management-approved game, and Johnson and pals were fired after one mess too many couldn't be explained. Fowl ball, Johnson claimed.

Today, there is a Poultry Bowler's Association, with membership in the several thousands nationally, to promote the sport, thus feathering their athletic nest. Several supermarkets have used it as a customer promotional event. Ahh, the gravy of greed.

One Hayduker, Skippy Windbreak II, says it's time to share this promotional effort with markets who haven't gotten into the game. "Don't be chicken," he says, adding, "There is no need to inform management first. Just do it!"

Now, moving from fowl to foul, here's a common supermarket scene. When some dense customer who can't count or is just plain rude barges into the 10 or less items express lane with a full cart, and most clerks are too chicken to say anything, help out. Drop some goodies from your cart into the offender's cart. Thank Pork Poovey for that one.

Pork also has a clever idea for the rude shopper who leaves a grocery cart in the middle of the isle while toddling off to the deli, for example. Pork says to casually move the offender's cart to another isle or out of the store completely. Then you come back and resume shopping.

Want to beat that "One To A Household" rebate limit? Ray Heffer says to make slight adjustments in the spelling of your last name on the rebate coupon. He adds, "Their computers are keyed to pick up only on your last name at a certain address. If you use variants it won't notice."

Thus, if your name is Gray, Heffer says to use Grey, Greay, Groy, Hrey, etc. Is a register receipt required? Send one from another time at the store.

Heffer also got angry at a store when it allowed one of its bagboys to get away with damaging Ray's car by sloppy cart management, i.e., the kid rammed Ray's vehicle on purpose.

Buy some canned sealant, Ray says. When you have the cart outside, quickly and carefully spray some of the sealant on the axle of only one front wheel. It will dry quickly and stickily, and it will make the cart pull hard to the right or left, depending upon which axle you did.

When Steve worked in a California supermarket, he was unfortunate to have to work with a racial bigot whom the store refused to discipline. So Steve did it for and to them.

The bigot's job was to stack the pet food. Steve used a razor knife to slit the very bottom seams of the 50-pound bags of dry dog food. The bigot would pick them up, and FLLOOOSHH, the bag bottom would fall out and so would 50 pounds of dog chow. Steve didn't do them all, just enough to make the bigot paranoid.

"The idiot spilled four bags before his peabrain kicked in. Management chewed his ass over that," says Steve, who also later did this same stunt to the bigot when he was loading canned food.

This made a louder noise and attracted more management attention.

Happily, management eventually got the point and the bigot was fired. I wonder if anyone burned a watermelon on his lawn that night in celebration?

SWEETIES

The topper comes from fabled feminist Mary Ann Barnes, who gaily and flamboyantly uncloseted her lesbianism in her bestselling book, *Men: Can't Live With 'Em, So We Don't.* Mary Ann shriveled a macho critic by telling him, "When they circumcised you, sonny, they threw away the wrong piece."

Michele tells the story about hapless Diane, who was gently scammed by a fun-loving ex-sweetie. When Diane said she didn't need to waste her money on needless things like perfume or deodorant, the guy told her, "Just use baking soda under your arms, then put some vanilla extract under there too, on your wrists and between your boobs."

I am sure you can imagine that effect and appearance. Michele says that Diane's smarts rank right down there with pocket lint.

Michele's other story involves the ex-spouse who just won't let go, going from promising to pleading to threatening to harassing, on and on . . . just won't quit.

"You keep the ex's address as long as you can, even

if it involves changing it a couple of times. The secret is to have access to the spouse's mail for as long as possible. That way you can pitch out his or her bills, tax notices, etc."

Ahhhh, Michele's March of the Sugar Dunning Scaries.

In another refrain of the same deadbeat dirge, Claudia and Tiffany had a recently divorced friend whose physically abusive former husband refused to pay his child support or alimony. The lady went to the shop he managed to demand her court-awarded money. He refused, so she made a small scene. He physically tossed her out the door.

The following day she appeared in front of the store with a poster that read, MY ABUSIVE EX-HUSBAND WON'T PAY HIS CHILD SUPPORT OR ALIMONY. He came out and threatened her in front of a growing crowd. He then threatened to call the police.

As he did that, she had a friend call the local TV station. Amazingly, the police and the camera crew arrived at the same time. It was quite a circus for the local evening news.

The next day the ex-husband received a telephone call from the shop's owner giving him hell for embarrassing the store's reputation, then giving him two options: pay or be fired. He paid.

The last of the fabled Puritans, Alter Kocker, wanted to pay back a friend with some humor over a double date that had gone awry. His friend was somewhat paranoid and insecure about his lady love.

Alter had a friend who could sound just like his pal's lady love. So, Alter had his friend call the guy and pretend to be lady love. She sounded pretty drunk, and Alter had party noise in the background. She kept giggling and saying things like "Stop that! Ohhh, not now, not yet," while she talked. Basically, she told the boyfriend that he was awesome in bed the night before and he could do that to her (and here she got clinically detailed) anytime. She giggled like lady love and hung up.

The real kicker is that Alter knew his pal had been home alone the night in question.

The School Slut seduced Serena's virginal boyfriend just to piss off Serena, a nasty habit of the slut, it seems. So, Serena took a very recognizable picture of the slut smoking a joint while in her cheerleader uniform.

She self-published 100 posters of that photo featuring a large headline that said, BOYS . . . DON'T EVER LET THIS HAPPEN TO YOUR DICK!! and posted them in all of their high school's wall areas, rooms, and teen hangouts.

In the same sense, one of Stormbringer's lady friends found out that her boyfriend was playing consenting sex games with a very nasty other woman. She did several funnies to her former boyfriend, all with the Good Hayduking Seal of Approval.

What she did to the other woman should bring the glass ceiling crashing down around the canard of The Sisterhood, and I don't mean nuns. Stormbringer's friend mixed up a diluted batch of Liquid Heat, the stuff athletes use to flame apart twisted muscles, and added it to the woman's douche. She also planned to place what fiberglass she hadn't used on her ex-boyfriend into the tampons of this by now literally scarlet woman.

Using a car to hassle or surveil a cheating sweetie is intrusive and costly, can be traced easily, and often results in police being summoned. The Amityville Horror II offers this wonderfully simple tradecraft tip: use a bicycle.

However, once when the Amityville Horror II wanted to play paranoia with her former sweetie, she would park her car in front of his home for as long as the law would allow. She would park it, take a cab or bus to work, to shop, or whatever, then retrieve it before the towing or ticketing deadline.

She said the guy had left her for a bimbo and had stuck her with unpaid bills and other problems. Amityville said she heard that the bimbo was physically afraid and that the ex-sweetie begged the police for help. He got no help nor sympathy.

A young friend of the Chaos Kid got scarred emotionally by a more experienced woman who took him hard for money and feelings. Being in school, this broad still lived at home. The Kid picked a time to call her parents when he knew she and some girlfriends had gone on mall patrol. Here's how the conversation went:

Chaos Kids (in adult voice): "Hello. Is this the (mark's last name) residence?"

Mark's parents: "Yes it is."

CK (very angrily): "Look, I don't care how old your daughter is or even if you care that she's the town slut. But, damn it, keep her and her boyfriends' away from my yard. She and that punk are out there fornicating on my lawn now. Think I can't see them? Well, I can, and so can my kids. This is your last warning!"

Chaos Kid then hung up.

SWIMMING POOLS

Certain blotchy neighbors of The Chicken Man kept trying to get him into trouble with the local police for no real reason. They had another weakness, other than picking on the wrong guy, i.e., a swimming pool.

Phenothailene is a fine, talc-like powder. It can be used as a cell dye in medical research, and it is also a powerful laxative. It can be ingested, inhaled, or absorbed through the skin. It is very potent. It will dissolve in alcohol but not water.

Chicken Man dissolved a batch and tossed the solution into the nasty folks' pool just before the cretins had equally buttwipe friends in for a pool party. Chicken says several guests sported a neat dye job, while most all had a bad case of the runs within two hours.

Floorwax Fran from Denver wanted to create an eerie feeling for a semimark's pool party, so she put a lot of dry ice in the pool. Great producer of long-lasting fog. Scared the guests, so she did.

When some nasty bullies were cruel to her kids, Barbara from Phoenix via good old KFYI told about tossing several motor-oil-filled balloons into the bullies' family pool. She also suggested alternative fillers for the balloons, too. Propriety forbids me from sharing these with you, however.

Master Zimmy worked for a jerk who bragged about his pool, which he could afford because he underpaid and overworked kids, then fired them if they complained. Living in a coastal fishing area, Zimmy had access to a large supply of fish entrails.

"I thought this buttwipe needed some organic matter in his pool, so I stocked it with lots and lots of fish guts while he was at work," Zimmy reported.

Zimmy says the turd came home from work, put on his bathing costume, and leaped right into the guts-laden pool. There was a loud scream and the mark was heard depooling, then barfing. He missed three days of work.

If marks would only stay within their own gene pool, they'd eventually down-breed to nuisance weeds.

TELEPHONES

AT&T's public-relations suitpeople spent major bucks helping media types shoot cholesterol levels long distance during the 1992 Democratic convention in America's favorite free-fire zone, New York City. According to their own statistics, their media lounge provided 4,300 top-grade hot dogs, 350 feet of weiner rolls, and 11,900 gallons of premium beer . . . all free for our independent mediaspinners.

Meanwhile, what of the rest of us? Has Caller ID got your number? Is your sense of privacy invaded? Ray Heffer to the rescue. Heffer found out from a friendly mole in the CO (that's Belljargon for Central Office) that if you punch in *67 before making your call, you will prevent the transmission of your telephone number. If you have a rotary phone, dial 1167 to block Caller ID.

It's also fun for your voice to do the talking while your mark is doing the paying. Iron Cross had a former friend who began to make nasty and harassing calls. Before taping and reporting the abuse to the police, Iron decided some literal payback was in order.

"I took my little Radio Shack one-piece phone with its alligator clip terminals to the guy's apartment house. I went into the utilities room and found the phone company's gray junction box.

"Because some kind installer had neatly keyed the apartment numbers to the appropriate terminals, I was able to quickly hook my clips, red and yellow, to the proper red and yellow wires of my mark," Iron explains.

Many of his calls were of the 900 variety, but he did make many prearranged late night calls to friends at pay phones or at work where the calls would be impossible to trace or track.

"One of my favorites was a truly hot 900 sexual line that charged $4.99 a minute for real sex talk. Over a week's period I ran up about $230 with them."

Thanks to Doug Brunnell I finally heard the wonderful Mushacia tape. It is hilarious; the man is a comic genius. The Mushacia tape is the ultimate in telecomedy harassment. If anyone knows who Mushacia is and/or the story of that tape, please let me know. I laughed until I nearly whet me knickers.

Here is a wonderful telephone conversation that should take place sometime around 3 A.M., according to its originator, Biggus. Y is YOU, M is MARK.

Y: Hello? What do you want?

M: (hopefully groggy) Huh? What? Who is this? What?

Y: Why did you call me at 3 A.M.? Who is this?

M: (awake now) What? You called me . . .

Y: (interrupting) Yeah, right. Funny. What's up? Who is this?

M: You called me. I didn't call you. Who is this?

Y: Hey, I'm working tomorrow. Who is this? I'm calling the police and the phone company about you, pal.

M: But, wait . . . who . . .

Y: (loudly) Fuck you, pal, and your mother! Don't ever call me again. (hang up)

You might also wish to heed Heffer's advice about *67.

Toronto's Naomi has a great gag for your mark. Call your mark from a pay phone and identify yourself as a phone company service person. Give him a bunch of jargon with lots of numbers and phone company lingo in it, but basically saying that you're doing line testing for the next three hours. Tell the mark specifically NOT to answer the phone regardless of how much it rings.

Then, as you go about your business for the next hour, call the mark from a pay phone every five minutes or so. Let it ring 15 times. Hang up. For the finale, call the mark again and just walk away . . . let the phone ring for half an hour if the mark's stupid enough to allow it.

Call the mark the next day and repeat the process.

When Marcel gets a stupid, inconsiderate wrong number caller, he never corrects this unwitting mark. He simply plays along. Once he got an irate husband who thought he'd called his wife's lover. Marcel never corrected him; instead, he insulted him and finally invited him "over" to settle it man to man. Marcel never knew the outcome of that one.

Amy once worked for Southern Bell. She says if you glue the mark's phone connect/disconnect button down just far enough, it won't show nor will it connect. Thus, the phone will keep ringing and ringing and ringing despite how often the mark "answers" the phone.

You call a company and get put on hold. No permanent hold for you; follow Mycroft Holmes' lead of calmly pushing the hold button on your phone. Then, using another line, dial the other party. When they answer, put them on hold. Mycroft thinks that you might be able to tie up their entire system if you just keep recycling the process.

Nimrod's neighbor used to play the stereo loud and late in one of those paper-thin-walled apartments so popular with cheap landlords. After no avail with polite requests, Nimrod got one of those superloud exterior phone bells like they use on construction sites. He mounted it to his bedroom wall facing toward where he knew the head of his neighbor's bed was.

"He slept during my day shift, so I would call myself from work four or five times a day and let that loud sucker ring for 15 or 20 times each," Nimrod noted. "Within the week he had turned down his stereo at night."

Once some idiot woke up Sal with a 2 A.M. wrong-number call to his girlfriend Betsy. He thought Sal was her brother, Joey. So Sal pretended to be Joey. He told the guy he'd go get Betsy. In two minutes Sal came back and told the guy that Betsy would be right there.

Five minutes later, Sal picked up the phone breathing heavily and said, "Ahhhh, sorry for the delay, pal. When I woke her up, my sister and I got hot and she's giving me head right now . . . she'll call you back when I'm done doing her!"

Sal hung up without waiting for a reply.

TELEVANGELIST

Father Skatapedo was so angry, his eyes could have cracked open clam shells at 100 meters. He was talking to a parishioner who'd just advised his elderly mother to give her life savings to one of the televangelist swindlers that gullible and elderly insomniacs flock to on satellite TV.

"Everyone has the right to be stupid, but you have abused the privilege," Father Skatapedo said, biting of each word like a bullet. Then, shaking his head, he muttered, "Jesus, Mary, and Haile Selassie!"

Ahhh, the true believers, the faithful who write Oral Roberts a check while breathing noisily through their pious mouths, their saliva bubbling with the mental effort. And, as Pat Robertson added, "Yeah, let the profits come unto me."

The Reverend Jonas Nightingale has prepared a list of questions to be asked of all televangelists before sending them worldly goods. One of Jonas' good disciples is our own Biggus Piraphicus. These questions might also be asked of any right-wing religious fascist:

- What were the Virgin Mary's measurements?
- Was Jesus well hung?
- Does God use condoms?
- Who is Lisa of Nazareth?
- Why does the Bible advocate oral sex?
- Would you rather have sex with a goat or a Navy SEAL?

Some of the fundamentalist street preachers get scary, too. When Captain Chaos gets attacked by them, he immediately begins to hector them back with a screaming attack of Islamic fundamentalism that he learned during a year's navy assignment in the Persian Gulf. To beat boredom, he'd studied the radical fundamental aspects of that religion, and he could use it quite effectively against our homegrown variety.

The Georgia Butler told me about a lady friend of his who was once verbally assaulted by some street preacher named Jed Smoot. She was in running clothes and old Jed called her a "harlot and whore" as she passed by his street corner congregation.

She stopped, looked at Jed's crotch, smiled, and in her best Debra Winger voice, purred, "Ohhh, and I've made you get a hard-on, haven't I, Jed? I didn't know you even had one."

She got an ovation. Jed was stymied. So was his stupored stiffie.

Mick Emm's aunt wasted a lot of money with some thieving televangelist who lie-promised to cure her arthritis. Mick and some friends borrowed some hymnals from the studio/church of the offending thief. They whited out the hymn numbers (hymns are numbered individually in a system that has nothing to do with page numbers). Then, using printed numbers, they renumbered about a third of the hymns. Nothing matched in any of the books. Mick Emm and friends returned the hymnals the following week. Television taping had to be stopped because of the musical chaos during hymn singing time.

Mick Emm says, "About 20 percent of the folks were singing totally different hymns . . . yet everyone was turned to Hymn 204, or whatever old Slimeass had chosen. The confusion was wonderful."

Consider what happened when they pass the collection plate in any of these Church of the Charlatan chapters, as Sal did when he contributed several coin pack condoms, the ones individually wrapped in heavy gold foil.

Once offered communion in a money-grabber church, Prairie Dog told them that his church allowed only one sacrament for communion. They asked him who and what. He held up a Flavour Aide pack and replied, "People's Temple, want a drink?"

Which is probably why there are dyslexic theologians who argue about the existence of dog.

URINE

The Louisiana Tchapatulas Trickster pissed on an incompetent professional who killed an innocent animal through drunken incompetence. It was a pisser of revenge as Trickster explains, "I bought a 10-gallon plastic container, which friends and I used as a urinal for as much of the summer as it took to fill it and to let it steep in the California sun.

"By six weeks there were new odors and life forms not known to this Earth coming from that bottle. We glued a plastic cork in the opening, then drilled a hole in the cork and attached a hose to it, down into that unspeakable.

"We leaned the bottle upside down at his expensive condo doorstep when we knew he was out to dinner with friends. The hose ran under the door . . . gravity did the rest."

When Trickster drove by the targeted condo the next morning all of the windows were open, there was a cleaning crew busy, and a carpet company truck was just arriving.

Savage Henry continues his urinary track to go after his mark with ice cubes (100-percent urine) attacks. Henry freezes his urine into over-sized cubes, which he uses to bombard his mark's redwood deck, flowers, garden, etc. The hot sun melts the ice and the uric acid does the rest.

General Jens once briefed me on how amusing it is to place those deodorant bricks from restaurant urinals on a hot radiator or wood burner. No, you don't steal used bricks! Buy them from a restaurant supply house.

A friend of Terry Moore told me about some lowlifes from a neighborhood nuisance bar coming outside and peeing in the alley between their dump and his family restaurant. Gentle negotiations failed, as did attempts to interest the local police in helping.

Terry's friend wired a 220-volt steel plate on the ground on his side of the property line. Instant success . . . hot-wired johnsons.

UTILITIES

Bill from Atlanta was owed some major money by a major deadbeat who was living up to his name. So, Bill decided that in addition to going after the guy legally, he would have some fun, too. For starters, Bill knew some contractors and was able to get the proper codes and jargon to pull off what he did.

"I had all of this deadbeat's utilities switched at the central office from his actual home to a new home that was under construction. The utility companies thought it was his new home. It wasn't," Bill said, adding that a settlement was eventually reached.

Feeling that simply cutting or transferring utility service is too mundane, The Rubber Fox has bills sent to a "temporary new address for the next three months." This always creates fun, as the new address is always some empty house, a secondary mark, a remailing service, a satanic cult, biker clubhouse, etc.

Before some PC Nazi skewers me for creating problems for "the innocent utility companies," let me remind

you that your quote is an oxymoron. If you don't under-
stand that, then you're half of one.

Pyro tells us that tampering with an electric meter is
a very big legal no-no, not to mention physically dangerous. But, if someone who knew what s/he was doing
would clip the seal, set the meter back, close it, then in-
expertly "repair" the clipped seal, the on-site resident
would be blamed.

Interestingly, Pyro, who used to work for a utility,
tells me that some very poor folks use strong magnets
stuck to their electric meters to slow down those little
metallic wheels that spin faster and faster as you use
more juice. Using a magnet to slow the wheels "reads"
less electricity than is actually being used, and that
means lower bills. This is also known as fraud.

That's what he had in mind when Mr. Coster says you
can attach magnets to your mark's meter just before the
service person arrives to read for billing. That way it will
look as if the mark is trying to defraud the company. Mr.
Coster's friend did this while the mark was on vacation, so
it looked as if he'd been stealing power for awhile.

Mr. Coster also says you can open the case, remove
the meter, then reinsert it upside down. This will make
those meter wheels run backward. Does that mean that
the utility company will owe you money?

Finally, old friend You Know Who decided to paint
over the mark's meter to make it tough to read. The service people were not pleased and the mark suffered because they charged him to install a new meter. You
Know waited another month, then poured water into the
new one.

Keep on Hayduking!

VIDEOS

Considering that most VCRs now have an audio dub feature, why not take Bucko's advice and dub the soundtrack of some porn flick over the video of the mark's nice home/family tapes or selected commercial ones? This would work in a mark's home, in a social situation, or in a situation using display or sales videos. It would work great for inspirational and other typical seminar videos as well.

Can't you just see it? Bucko can. The entire Mark family is setting around on a popcorn Sunday afternoon screening "Old Yeller" when the soundtrack suddenly changes to some sexy, hot female or male voice screaming, "Fuck Me! Oh, fuck me, _____ (Mark's or spouse's or kids' name go here)" while the video plays on. I thought it was a fun idea. But, we'll fast forward.

Video rental places that allow you to select your own tapes always place a security strip on the tape. Usually, it's a silvery metallic tape with a checkerboard design. Attempting to leave with a purloined video with tape attached sets off a microwave beam that makes lots of noise.

Knowing this, Heffer suggests that when you rent tapes, remove the alarm stickers, then reattach them to your mark or to his clothing or accessories. That way, when mark goes into any store with this security system, the alarms will go off like crazy. Embarrassment!! Frustration!! Anger!! Many laughs for you!!

SN 2470 had a run-in with a video store that charged him an extra day's rental even though he'd returned his video on the day it was due. He'd put it in their after-hours slot, like at a library. He argued, but paid, then vowed that he'd pay back, too.

He adds that the store owner had a reputation for being nasty to customers and for cheating folks in other ways.

So, our friend got an empty video box from the shop, placed two large magnets in it, and Superglued it shut. He put his little magnetic bomb in the drop box just after the store closed for a holiday so that two days would elapse between damage and discovery.

Magnets cause all sorts of problems with video recording. According to a report in the local newspaper, two dozen tapes were damaged by his magnetic bomb. That's rude, SN 2470, but so deserved, and done so well.

In keeping with his desire to help his fellow citizens, Captain Skellen says to learn what brand of television set your mark has. Then, by properly setting the DIP switches in your remote, you might be able to help him change channels a lot. And, if you're persistent, you can probably override or alter his attempts to come back to his favorite show.

I can't wait to share this idea with Elaine the Master Clicker.

VOMIT

Vomit, that famous wet, multihued, plaid belch, is a wonderful and useful armament in your revenge arsenal. For quicky starters, Biggus came up with the idea of vomiting into Ziploc freezer bags that had been marked as stew, then storing same in your mark's freezer.

Old pal Barfo and Miss Marsha came up with a wonderful recipe involving our useful friend, vomitus. Uncle George had eaten an entire sponge cake baked with love and care by Ann Marie. Even so, he became quite ill, probably because he'd followed the cake with several six packs of Yerg's Ripest to quell his massive thirst.

Uncle George announced his plans to hurl.

Barfo and Miss Marsha got out the mixing bowls for Uncle George to fill, which he so graciously did. It looked just like cake batter, except for the remnants of his dinner, including some chunks of potato.

Barfo and Miss Marsha put the "batter" into little cake pans and baked it for the bad boys at a competing saloon nearby. Uncle George delivered the still warm cakes to the barflies who scarfed them down.

Barfo, Miss Marsha, Ann Marie, and Uncle George had a great belly laugh about this.

OK, so you can't stomach producing your own vomit. Thanks to Warhawk, we now have instant designer vomit that's microwaveable. Here's his recipe. Use TOTAL oatmeal and make it into a thick, goopy paste. Nuke it for 30 seconds at high. Add Karo syrup and Heinz ketchup (substitute chili sauce for a very vile odor), and nuke all of this at high for 20 or 30 seconds.

Place in a plastic bag to strengthen and retain the odor, Warhawk says. Then apply within the next couple of hours. He says it is truly vile and odorous.

Finally, for both an international flavor and to inculate some culture into this tome, my friend Eduardo from Cabo San Lucas told me that the Mexican version of projectile vomiting is known as "Calling the Monster." Think about it—the sound, the body motions . . . it's perfect.

WATER CLOSET

Joe Ling has a pleasingly practical post-potty use philosophy: always wipe your hands before picking
your teeth, especially if you didn't have any toilet paper.

As the average citizen of any cultured nation is very
uncomfortable even hearing discussion of body waste
functions, these masses and fluids are valued armament
for you, as I noted in the VOMIT chapter.

"Imagine the chagrin of some poor citizen who sees
you seemingly reach into a toilet bowl, fish out a seemingly fresh piece of dump, and take a bite," is the rhetor-
ical question of Steve Wilson who, with a shit-eating
grin, explains.

"Make your own," he says. "Mix 2/3 chocolate and
1/3 butterscotch powdered puddings with about half the
milk that the instructions recommend.

"You can experiment for color and solidity, and also
add chopped nuts or corn kernel for texture and appearance. Pour the thickened mix onto a piece of waxed paper and roll into the classic log shape. Freeze until ready
for use and amusement," Steve suggests.

Some years ago when The Chicken Man was in the military, his unit owned a typical rednecked bully of an NCO. Chicken says guys used to take dumps in the guy's boondockers on nights they were sure to get a "call to battle," meaning up and dressed for instant action, including slamming on boots. It worked each time.

Perhaps Dick Smegma knew about this when he suggested that before creating fresh fecal matter for Hayduking purposes, it's well to ingest two tablespoons of Pepto Bismol. It clumps your dump and turns it dark black.

Smegma also conned a gullible telephone service person to list the name "Shithead" followed by his mark's phone number in a city directory. He told the clerk that the name was pronounced "Shy-thead," and proceeded to spell it as "Shi," then said "thead." It worked. He sent me a copy of the listing. The mark took a lot of abusive calls, and the phone company stalled on changing his number at its expense.

You'll laugh, but I know someone who tried this funny idea from Stormbringer. He says to get one of those conductive pens used to fix circuit boards. Run two thin lines from each outlet of a 120 AC socket to the toilet. Run one line up to and around half of the seat; do the same for the other. That way, both cheeks get juiced. Be careful! But it sounds like a great electric laxative to me.

The Paul W. Ass toilet seat look-alike stunt involved stringing an X frame of electrical tape across the commode opening, then fastening a 5x7 portrait of your mark in the center. It's amazing how many folks will use it and not remove it. One friend did this with a photo of an unpopular county commissioner at the county court house latrine, and dozens of employees sort of peed on the boss each day. Works unisex, too.

Reading what Allen P. Watkins did to a bus terminal

toilet when the terminal management soiled his suit and lost his luggage makes me wonder if public poop palaces will ever be safe havens again. Allen smuggled the bottom half of a seated mannequin into the facility's men's room along with a small cassette playback machine. He set the mannequin, complete with lowered pants, as if it were a person using the stall. The tape player had an endless loop with loud, obnoxious, and graphic sound effects of flatus, excretion, belching, gasping, and sighing.

But, as Allen says, he also thought of putting two mannequin lowers, presumably face to face, in one stall with a sexually explicit tape. He also said to superglue the stall door shut.

A further refinement might be to have a female friend slip a unit into the ladies' room featuring either male activity. Or a female voice in the men's room.

As much fun as they are, you have to wonder how the old WC got such an unpleasant reputation. It wasn't my fault.

WEDDINGS

Here are two social tips that we can thank the
Gorch Brothers, Lyle and Tector, for providing
us. If you are asked where the bride is registered, it is
not appropriate to reply, "The American Kennel Club."
And a bridal veil made of plastic window screening is
not only inexpensive, it's also a proven fly deterrent, a
major plus for weddings held in certain geographical areas or among certain ethnic groups.

By the way, the Gorch Brothers are major patrons of
the arts in Lemhi County, Idaho, where they serve on the
Salmon Arts Council and with the Lemhi Arts Council.

Doing his bit for the homeless, Mike from LA printed
500 extra wedding reception invitations for his mark's
daughter's big day. He offered a free, all-you-can-eat
buffet on the invitations, which he handed out the morning of the wedding at homeless shelters and soup
kitchens. There was an outside buffet after the wedding,
and the extra guests did show up. Most of them got a
goodly amount of food in the confusion before the police arrived.

Mojo Nuchshlepper did the same scam, only he invited outlaw biker club members and the city's rival gangs. A lot more police officers had to come to this one.

Biggus Piraphicus has two wedding presents for us today. One is to wrap a kinky sex toy without a card. This works well for a wedding shower as well as a baby shower for a mother-to-be. Biggus' other present, which he saw done once, was to arrange a slippery metallic shim under the tablecloth that will tilt the wedding cake enough to topple it on the bride and groom at a prearranged signal.

The Renegade must have gone to the same wedding. He once left a wrapped dead rabbit on the present table, to be opened at the reception, of course. Only he left a card . . . from a secondary mark, an old flame of the bride, who was at the event. Not only is it gross, but there is also a subtle message there, i.e., "the rabbit died." Get it?

Renegade also had a friend go through the reception line. He was unshaven and scruffy, chewing tobacco, and badly needed a bath. He open-mouth kissed the bride and tried to get his tongue and the chew into her mouth. A lot of it dribbled on her gown. He split in the confusion. Renegade, who was there, laughed. The bride was a #10 bitch, you see.

Lastly, after many years of attending the weddings of friends, then the next marriage for the same friends, and sometimes ditto for the third time, plus their kids, I have some wedding suggestions of my own:
- No matter how overheated you get on the dance floor, never remove your underwear there.
- However, when dancing with the mother of the bride, it is quite acceptable to blow your nose on her shoulder.

- Offer to show guests photos of the bride being intimate with a farm animal.
- Offer to show guests photos of the groom being intimate with the bride's father.
- In the receiving line, hand the bride some Binaca and tell her it will kill the taste of the cum. Or do the same for the bride's mother. Or father.
- Flashing a realistic badge, demand that guests show you their invitations. You might even wish to lead away a bewildered guest as if under arrest.
- Just after the bride throws her garter, perhaps a few friends could start chanting, "Show us your tits!"
- Pretending to be inebriated, fall onto the food table and/or into the cake.
- Plant drugs on the bride and groom or in their car. Then, be a good citizen and inform the authorities.
- Openly display drugs on the food table.

After attending some of these weddings, I wonder if, in the big picture, these couples might not be better off just buying salad shooters, toasters, and other latent garage-sale inventory and staying single.

THE LAST WORD

L etters. That's the last word in each of my books
Please write to me, as I am always glad to hear
from friends, new readers, and other Haydukers who
have funny stunts and stories to share. If you have something hilarious that you want me to share in a future
book, please let me know in your letter.

Most all of the people whose names appear in my
books are real people, even if their names are not. You
are encouraged to select a penname for yourself and let
me know that, too.

I personally answer all of my own mail; I really do.
But, as I do travel a lot, I'm not always prompt to respond. Please be patient. Also, if you want me to write
back, you'll have to include a real address, too.

I cannot promise when your stunt will get into one
of my future books. There are too many variables for
that. But I do keep my promises.

One thing I don't keep is any file or record of your
letters, names, or addresses. For that reason, please include your name and address with each letter.

Please write to:
George Hayduke
P.O. Box 1307
Boulder CO 80306-1307

THANK YOU! THANK YOU! AND GOODNIGHT . . .
YOU'VE BEEN A GREAT AUDIENCE. GOODNIGHT. I
LOVE YOU!!!

LEGALIZE FREEDOM

More Humor Books From Carol Publishing Group!

Ask for the books listed below at your bookstore. Or to order direct from the publisher call 1-800-447-BOOK (MasterCard or Visa) or send a check or money order for the books purchased (plus $4.00 shipping and handling for the first book ordered and 50¢ for each additional book) to Carol Publishing Group, 120 Enterprise Avenue, Dept. 575, Secaucus, NJ 07094.

Advanced Backstabbing and Mudslinging Techniques by George Hayduke, paperback $7.95 (#40560)

The Best Book of Puns by Art Moger, paperback $7.95 (#51097)

The Business Disasters Book of Days by Jill Herbers, paperback $9.95 (#51585)

The Complete Pun Book by Art Moger, paperback $8.95 (#50776)

First, Kill All the Lawyers, compiled by Bill Adler, paperback $8.95 (#51587)

501 Survival Tips for Men: Making Your Way in a World Full of Women by Craig Hartglass, paperback $8.95 (#51504)

Getting Even by George Hayduke, oversized paperback $12.95 (#40314)

Getting Even 2 by George Hayduke, oversized paperback $12.95 (#40337)

Henny Youngman's Giant Book of Jokes, paperback $6.95 (#50854)

The Howard Stern Book by Jim Cegielski, paperback $12.95 (#51505)

How to be a Stand-up Comic by Richard Belzer, paperback $9.95 (#51319)

How to Make Your Analyst Love You by Theodor Saretsky, paperback $7.95 (#51412)

If New York City Was the World, by John Kerschbaum, paperback $8.95 (#51573)

It's Impossible to Learn Elevator Repair From Your Mother, by R.S. Bean, paperback $9.95 (#51327)

The Limerick paperback $14.95 (#50713)

Make 'em Pay by George Hayduke, paperback $7.95 (#40421)

Make My Day by George Hayduke, paperback $7.95 (#40464)

Mayhem by George Hayduke, paperback $7.95 (#40565)

More of the World's Best Dirty Jokes by Mr. "J", paperback $5.95 (#50710)

The North Dakota Joke Book by Mike Dalton, paperback $7.95 (#51041)

Revenge by George Hayduke, oversized paperback $14.95 (#40353)

Revenge Techniques From the Master by George Hayduke, paperback $8.95 (#40575)

Righteous Revenge by George Hayduke, paperback $8.95 (#40569)

The "Seinfeld" Aptitude Test, by Beth B. Golub, paperback $8.95 (#51583)

The 7 Habits of Highly Ineffective People: Low-Effort Lessons in Mismanaging for Success - A Parody by Herman Minor paperback $8.95 (#51582)

Some Day My Prince Will Come: A Guide for Women Whose Dream Has Not Yet Come True by Serena Gray, paperback $10.95 (#51510)

Still More of the World's Best Dirty Jokes by Mr. "J", paperback $3.95 (#50834)

201 Ways to Get Even With Your Boss by Linda Higgins, paperback $8.95 (#51570)

Underground Office Humor by S.E. Mills, paperback $9.95 (#51567)

The World's Best Jewish Humor by Stanley A. Kramer, paperback $8.95 (#51503)

The World's Dirtiest Dirty Jokes by Mr. "J", paperback $7.95 (#51478)

The World's Greatest Golf Jokes by Stan McDougal, paperback $6.95 (#50831)

Prices subject to change; books subject to availability